1,000,000 Books

are available to read at

www.ForgottenBooks.com

Read online
Download PDF
Purchase in print

ISBN 978-1-333-51736-6
PIBN 10514413

This book is a reproduction of an important historical work. Forgotten Books uses
state-of-the-art technology to digitally reconstruct the work, preserving the original format
whilst repairing imperfections present in the aged copy. In rare cases, an imperfection in
the original, such as a blemish or missing page, may be replicated in our edition. We do,
however, repair the vast majority of imperfections successfully; any imperfections that
remain are intentionally left to preserve the state of such historical works.

Forgotten Books is a registered trademark of FB &c Ltd.
Copyright © 2018 FB &c Ltd.
FB &c Ltd, Dalton House, 60 Windsor Avenue, London, SW19 2RR.
Company number 08720141. Registered in England and Wales.

For support please visit www.forgottenbooks.com

1 MONTH OF FREE READING

at

www.ForgottenBooks.com

By purchasing this book you are eligible for one month membership to ForgottenBooks.com, giving you unlimited access to our entire collection of over 1,000,000 titles via our web site and mobile apps.

To claim your free month visit: www.forgottenbooks.com/free514413

* Offer is valid for 45 days from date of purchase. Terms and conditions apply.

English
Français
Deutsche
Italiano
Español
Português

www.forgottenbooks.com

Mythology Photography **Fiction** Fishing Christianity **Art** Cooking Essays Buddhism Freemasonry Medicine **Biology** Music **Ancient Egypt** Evolution Carpentry Physics Dance Geology **Mathematics** Fitness Shakespeare **Folklore** Yoga Marketing **Confidence** Immortality Biographies Poetry **Psychology** Witchcraft Electronics Chemistry History **Law** Accounting **Philosophy** Anthropology Alchemy Drama Quantum Mechanics Atheism Sexual Health **Ancient History** **Entrepreneurship** Languages Sport Paleontology Needlework Islam **Metaphysics** Investment Archaeology Parenting Statistics Criminology **Motivational**

"Mexico has found her master at last."
Frontispiece. (See *Page* 59.)

ITURBIDE

A SOLDIER OF MEXICO

BY

JOHN LEWIN McLEISH, A.M., M.D.

THE

Abbey Press

PUBLISHERS

114

FIFTH AVENUE

London   NEW YORK   Montreal

955
M163
itu

TO

HIS EXCELLENCY

SÉNOR PORFIRIO DIAZ,

PRESIDENT OF THE REPUBLIC OF MEXICO,

THE AUTHOR DEDICATES

"ITURBIDE"

AS A TOKEN OF APPRECIATION

OF THE MANY COURTESIES SHOWN HIS FATHER,

THE LATE DR. JOHN McLEISH

OF SABINAL, CHIHUAHUA, MEXICO,

BY THE

MEXICAN GOVERNMENT

DURING THE YEARS 1890–1896.

J. L. McLEISH, M.D.

CINCINNATI, O., January 1st, 1900.

M679750

AUTHORITIES ON THE PERIOD.

(Consulted for " Iturbide.")

Lorenzo de Zavala: "Ensayo Historico de las Revoluciones de Mejico."

Pablo Mendivil: " Historia de Mejico."

Carlos Bustamente: "Cuadro Historico."

Agustino d'Iturbide: " Ensayo o breves Memorias."

Madame Calderon de la Barca: " Life in Mexico." .

Nicholas Mill, Esq.: " History of Mexico." (London, 1824.)

Philip Young: "Mexico." (1847.)

John Frost: " Pictorial Mexico."

William D. Robinson: " Memoirs of the Mexican Revolution."

Abbé Clavigero: "History of Mexico."

Blackwood's Magazine (1824): An Account of the Mexican Revolution, Viator.

University Magazine, N. Y., Feb.–March, 1894: Mexican Independence, J. L. McLeish.

J. M. L. Mora: Mejico y sus Revoluciones. (Paris, 1836.)

Brantz Mayer: Mexico Aztec, Spanish and Republican.

A. R. Thummel: Mexico und die Mexicaner. (Erlangen, 1848.)

iv   Authorities on the Period.

J. R. Poinsett, Esq. : Notes on Mexico.

S. Basch, M. D. : Recuerdos de Mexico.

Manuel Payno : El Libro Rojo. (Mexico, 1870.)

F. C. Gooch ; Face to Face with the Mexicans.

R. A. Wilson : Mexico and its Religion.

Dr. Lemprière : "Mexico."

W. E. Curtis : "The Capitols of Spanish America."

A. M. Gilliam ; Tablelands and Cordilleras of Mexico.

Col. G. S. Church : Historical and Political Review of Mexico.

M. Chevalier : Mexico, Ancient and Modern.

William Butler, D.D.: Mexico in Transition from the Power of Political Romanism to Civil and Religious Liberty.

DRAMATIS PERSONÆ

General Agustin de Iturbide, afterwards Emperor of Mexico.
General Antonio Lopez de Santa Anna. A Gentleman of
     Vera Cruz.
His Excellency Don Juan Apodaca, Viceroy of Mexico.
Captain la Garza, an Old-young Man.
Rafael Aristo, of the Society of Jesus.
Captain Berdejo, of the "Viceroy's Own."
His Eminence the Archbishop of Mexico.
An Innkeeper.
A Jailer.
Juana la Garza.
Dahalia Santa Anna.
Madame de Iturbide.
Mother Superior of the Convent of Santa Teresa.
Felicie.
       Ladies and Gentlemen of the Viceroy's Court.
       Officers, Troopers, Priests, Nuns, etc.

LIST OF ILLUSTRATIONS.

1. Mexico has found her master at last..........*Frontispiece.*
   T. Lunt.

PAGE

2. Don Augustino de Iturbide...........*T. Victor Hall.* 18
3. She was accredited the most beautiful woman in Mexico................................*A. E. Krehbiel.* 26
4. The lady Juana la Garza flung wide the door and looked at the wretched man who stood there, silent, grim and sorrowful..... ...*T. Victor Hall.* 62
5. A man and a woman lay, manacled to the floor....... 82
   T. Victor Hall.
6. "Open the secret panel of the Viceroys," replied the priest.........................*T. Victor Hall.* 124
7. Slowly the soldiers of the Blues retreated before the determined onset of Santa Anna. Etc........... 148
   T. Victor Hall.

Cover design by *T. Victor Hall.*

AUTHOR'S NOTE.

ONE day in the early nineties, the author was wandering through the stone paved, gloomy corridors of the Imperial Palace of Iturbide, and in a moment was born the germ of the story which has wrought itself out in "A Soldier of Mexico." The setting was drawn from ever present, loved memories of days and nights spent in the mountains of the interior and picturesque camp life on the endless stretch of chaparral covered desert. As these pages were penned, a vivid mind picture of the old world city in the New—Tenochtitlan—with its massive palaces and crumbling convents, was born again, a reminder of the days when fanatic priests, haughty viceroys, beautiful women, ardent lovers and dashing soldiers, played their parts upon the stage of Mexican history with that dramatic intensity which has ever characterized the children of the southland. The Latin races are essentially neurastheniacs. Like the French and Spaniards, the Mexicans are emotional to a degree that at times borders on the hysterical. It is theirs to love and hate with a depth possible only in so peculiarly constituted a people.

The author has endeavored to tell the story of "Iturbide" as a Mexican would tell it, and a story so told necessitates, perforce at times, a melodramatic rapidity of action and ultra intensity of the element of passion, consistent with the people and the setting.

J. L. M.

CONTENTS.

		PAGE
Historical Preface		15
I.	For Love of a Woman	21
II.	Juana la Garza	26
III.	A Mason at Sight	36
IV.	The Fête in Honor of the Viceroy	41
V.	The Million-Dollar Convoy of the Viceroy	50
VI.	The Bedchamber of Juana la Garza	61
VII.	The Honor of Santa Anna	68
VIII.	The Dungeons of San Juan de Uloa	80
IX.	For the Good of the Church of Rome	95
X.	The Conversion of a Woman-hater	105
XI.	The Compliments of General Santa Anna	117
XII.	The Compliments of the Emperor Iturbide	135
	Epilogue	155

HISTORICAL PREFACE.

(From the thesis, "The Rise and Fall of the First Empire in Mexico," submitted by the author to the trustees of Princeton University, for the degree of Master of Arts, conferred in June 1897.)

THERE are some chapters in Mexican history as yet unwritten. While there exist, it is true, many voluminous tomes, by such historians as Zarate, Bustamente, Zavala and others dealing with different epochs, in the story of the Southern Republic,—they are unreliable on account of prejudice and partiality. One must discriminate and combine in order to gain from their writings any concept approaching the truth.

The story of the Mexican people is a strangely pathetic one. It is the story of four centuries of struggle and revolution—the vacillating, fickle history of all Latin races. The first three hundred years of Mexican history can be read in the life stories of sixty-two Spanish Viceroys.

During those years, when the power of Spain was tottering to its downfall,—when the breaking of the Catholic coalition dealt a terrific blow to her old world resources, Spain endeavored to recuperate her energy, by

15

16 Historical Preface.

having recourse to the yet undeveloped riches of the New Spain—Mexico.

The firm, iron hand of Spanish Viceroy rule fell heavy on the Mexican people, and the whole period of Spanish Viceroy administration is marked by revolution after revolution.

The time for Independence was not yet rife however. A native historian writing of the latter days of Viceroy rule says:

" The condition of the people was a species of slavery, a necessary consequence of their condition,—of the ignorance in which they were maintained, of the terror which the authorities inspired by their military forces, of despotism and its attendant evils, and more than all of the Inquisition, sustained by military force and by the religious superstition of the clergy and rabid fanatics without methods of instruction. No useful truth, no principle, no maxim capable of inspiring noble or generous sentiments, were heard in the Jesuit schools. Three fourths of the population were indigent, without property, with no kind of occupation, without ever the hope of some day acquiring one—peopling the haciendas, ranches and mines of the wealthy proprietors."

As in Spain, where the whole power and political policy was subject to Church dictation, so in Mexico,—Mother Church ruled supreme. As the power of the clergy began to wane in the Old World, so gradually it endeavored to

Historical Preface. 17

regain its lost ascendancy in the New. Step by step priestcraft extended its sway over Mexico, and her Viceroys. To-day one can find on every side, reminiscences of the Inquisition and its despotic rule in Mexico.

It is with pleasure one turns from the period of Viceroy rule to the new order of things generated with the opening of the nineteenth century. The sixteenth of September, 1810, is a day as sacred to the Mexican heart as our own Fourth of July to us. It marks the first blow in behalf of Mexican Independence,—it marks the rising of a suffering and oppressed people against the grim, tyrannical power of old Spain—it marks the inchoation of a series of revolutions and uprisings which finally culminated in giving Mexico freedom from priestcraft and the old world Suzerainty of the Spanish Bourbons.

The proto-martyrs of Mexican Independence —Hidalgo, Allende, Aldama, Jimenez, Rayon, and Matamoras,—fell fighting for the cause in which they had taken up the sword.

For years and years the struggle went on, conducted by such men as Santa Anna, Guerrero, Guadalupe Victoria, and Bravo. For the Spaniards found it a hopeless task to crush the partisans of Liberty. Men had suddenly been awakened and roused to action by the intrepid warrior Hidalgo. They longed for the glorious prize for which he had laid down his life.

There now arose a central figure in the

18 Historical Preface.

struggle for Independence—a man endowed with unbounded ambition and unquestioned ability. His life history reads like a romance and is full of interest and incident. His career was as strange and brilliant as that of Napoleon Bonaparte. Its ending was as pathetic. Says the historian Zavala:

"Don Agustin de Iturbide, Colonel of a battalion of provincial troops, a native of Valladolid, was endowed with brilliant attainments and amongst other qualities of valor and activity out of the ordinary. Of average physique, he possessed the fortitude and endurance necessary for undergoing the greatest hardships of campaigning, and ten years of this continued exercise had strengthened his natural endurance. He had an active and self-assertive character and had observed that to remain in favor with the authorities it was necessary to be at a safe distance from those who could command him. It is indisputable that Iturbide was possessed of a superior intellect and that his ambition was founded on that high resolve which depreciates dangers and which no obstacles can restrain. He had familiarized himself with danger in battle. He had recognized the power of the Spanish arms and he was competent to measure the capacity of chiefs of both parties. It must be admitted that he did not deceive himself in the estimate which he formed of them all. He possessed the consciousness of his own superiority, and with this assurance he did not hesitate to place

Don Augustino de Iturbide.

Page 18.

Historical Preface. 19

himself at the head of a National party waiting only to gain the confidence of his fellow-countrymen."

Such is Zavala's estimate of Iturbide—the consummator of the great task begun by Hidalgo.

Truly no ordinary man was Agustin de Iturbide. With no little interest he had watched the movements of the insurgent chiefs—Santa Anna and the rest. He began to reflect. Spain was undeniably losing her hold upon Mexico. A change was imminent. Iturbide was a far-seeing man. He craved honor—military emolument—distinction. Spain, torn by internecine strife, trembling on the verge of a precipice could not for long maintain her foothold in Mexico. To satisfy his ambition, he must look elsewhere. For some years Iturbide had been formulating a plan of action which was to overthrow forever Spanish rule in Mexico. Astute and clever he simply bided his time—attaching to himself by a series of intrigues, men of all parties—ecclesiastical, military and political. When one considers his colossal undertaking, admiration gives way to surprise. His countrymen longed for Independence, and he made that the fundamental feature of his plan which he denominated Las Tres Garantias. To express his intentions he assumed the word Union. To conciliate the all-powerful clergy, he added Religion. To gain the sympathy of the people at

Historical Preface.

large, he chose the appellation, Independence. His idea was to overthrow forever Viceroy rule in Mexico and to create a home dynasty.

One man more than any other in Mexico could aid him in his design, General Antonio Lopez de Santa Anna, a wealthy young gentleman of Cruz Vera, and an intrepid soldier.

Iturbide met Santa Anna, and meeting him found the man whose sword was to lead him to a throne and whose voice was to be the first to cry that grito which meant the downfall of that New World Empire for which both had battled against the picked forces of Spain.

And of that the story.

THE AUTHOR.

ITURBIDE, A SOLDIER OF MEXICO

CHAPTER I.

FOR LOVE OF A WOMAN.

IT was a beautiful evening of February, 1821. Through the shaded plaza of the City of Mexico, near the grand Cathedral, a train of placid-faced, peaceful looking burros laden with great pulque-filled pigskins were trotting at a leisurely pace towards the southern barrier of the Capitol.

Lounging in the few *pulquerias* of the plaza, scarlet clad, dashing troopers and green-jacketed chasseurs embraced and quaffed their wine with many an oath as soldiers love to do.

In the great square, hibuscus, orchids and dahlias peeped out from the cacti and yucca.

It was the hour of the Angelus. Troopers and chasseurs stood immobile, with bared heads and uplifted glasses. The old fruit-woman, at the door of the Cathedral, fell upon her knees beside her pomegranate stand and crossed herself repeatedly, while her lips

22 Iturbide, A Soldier of Mexico.

moved in prayer. But if the hands and lips of the old fruit-woman were occupied with her rosary, her eyes were not. She looked with horror upon a tall and slender gentleman, of a military bearing, despite the long black manto completely enveloping his uniform—she looked with horror upon this gentleman who walked calmly down the plaza at the hour of the Angelus, with his sombrero upon his head. "An accursed heretic," she thought, and continued her prayer to the Blessed Virgin.

The stranger took his stand near one of the great towers of the Cathedral and drawing his manto the more closely around him, became almost as immobile as one of the statues of the Saints in the niches above him,

From the great doors of the Cathedral, the throng of worshipers began to come out, singly and in pairs. They were mostly women. Those of the better classes had their faces coquettishly hidden in their silk rebosas.

Among the last to issue forth was a slender, graceful young woman, clad in black, her features entirely concealed by a dainty silk rebosa. In her hand she carried a prayer-book.

The man in the black manto took a forward step, and with the graceful bow of a gallant, swept the ground with his sombrero.

"Dahalia," he murmured softly.

The girl shrank back against one of the great columns and turned upon him a white pitiful, tear-stained face in which love and fear were both expressed.

For Love of a Woman. 23

"Dios, how beautiful you are!" murmured the man passionately. And then more softly.

"Dahalia, can you forgive me for seeking you despite my promise? You are indispensable to me—you have become a veriest part of myself—give me once more the assurance of your love and I will aid your brother in his struggle for Mexican liberty—yes, and here in the shadow of the Cathedral, I swear to you that I will take up my sword in the same cause. For your love I will forget that I ever swore allegiance to the Royalist cause, forget that I am Colonel of a regiment baptized with the blood of your countrymen and mine; for the first time in my life will I forswear myself——"

The girl shook her head and the man continued more earnestly :—

"Ah, do not turn from me, dear one. I have periled my liberty, perhaps my life, in coming here. And all for love of you, my darling,—all for love of you. I fancy His Excellency the Viceroy would not take it lightly that the Colonel of a Royal Regiment conversed with the sister of one of the proscribed——"

"With the sister of Santa Anna,—a man who is as much a patriot as you are a tyrant. Ah, no, Colonel Iturbide, you do well to remind me of the difference in our stations. And I will no longer peril the precious life of the butcher of my people. Draw not your sword for our cause but keep it for the service of His Excellency. Adios, señor Colonel Iturbide.

24   Iturbide, A Soldier of Mexico.

It is far, far better that we part, and far better would it have been had we never met."

And she drew her rebosa more closely around her, turning from him.

But he caught her slender wrist and said hurriedly, passionately,

"Ah, Dahalia,—you are cruel—my niña. When you came to the Court of the Viceroy in the suite of the Lady La Garza, I saw you and I loved you. You repulsed me."

"Si, señor Colonel. Because a sister of the rebel Santa Anna could only bring ruin upon the favorite of the Viceroy. Had you not been a persecutor of my people—of my Mexico— then—perhaps—but no. It could not be. I came to the Viceroy's court upon a secret mission,—a mission of death."

"Of death?" gasped the man in black.

"Ah si—to strike you down in the salon of His Excellency and avenge, with one quick stroke of the stiletto, my poor countrymen— slaughtered by your troops—to avenge Hidalgo and his little band of consecrated patriots— to enable my dear brother to uprear the red, white and green banner of the Mexicans, over that accursed emblem—the banner of old Spain, —the blood-reddened flag of the Bourbons. But I was only a simple girl—a niña, señor,— and I—I could not help loving you, and——"

"Ah, Dahalia,—my chiquita—— "

And he would have caught her in his arms, but she waved him back gently.

"Your promise!" she murmured.

For Love of a Woman. 25

"Dahalia—when I promised to remain away from your presence until you yourself should tell me to return, I did not realize what I was doing. Ah, chiquita—my love for you is greater than my pride. It is killing me. To-night I could bear the agony of separation no longer. And even at the cost of the Viceroy's displeasure, I have come to you again."

"You were wrong, Colonel mine," murmured the girl reproachfully. "When the lady Juana La Garza denounced me before the Viceroy as the sister of the rebel Santa Anna and forced me to flee the Vice-regal Palace and hide a refugee in the purlieus of the Capitol, it was not prudent for a man so well known as the trusted officer of His Excellency to——"

"But a trusted officer of His Excellency's no longer," broke in her companion. "For love of a woman, Iturbide perjures himself and betrays the trust of the Bourbons."

"And for love of a woman, Santa Anna walks into the spider's web," broke in a calm, half sneering voice.

The girl turned quickly with a half audible cry.

"Ay de mi—my brother—and in the Capitol —this is madness indeed."

Then fell fainting into the arms of the newcomer.

CHAPTER II.

JUANA LA GARZA.

SHE was a wee little thing, with a wealth of wavy, golden hair and great blue eyes, lips cherry red and voluptuous, hands slender and delicate, laden with costly jewels. From under her rich, satin skirts peeped out a dainty slipper, indicating an attractive little foot.

She was accredited the most beautiful woman in Mexico, but there was a hardness about her mouth—the satanic hardness of a wiler of men—and at times from those pretty blue eyes shot a steely glint that bespoke either much passion or much wickedness. Quien sabe?

On this February evening the lady Juana la Garza, reclined lazily upon a divan in her richly furnished boudoir, at Casa Garza. A sort of feline smile played upon her pretty red lips and she presented a picture of delicious abandon in her delicate evening dress.

From an adjoining apartment came the sweet strains of the Palace band.

For the lady Juana la Garza entertained this evening in honor of His Excellency, the Viceroy of Mexico, Don Juan Apodaca, and she waited only the first notes of the Hymno

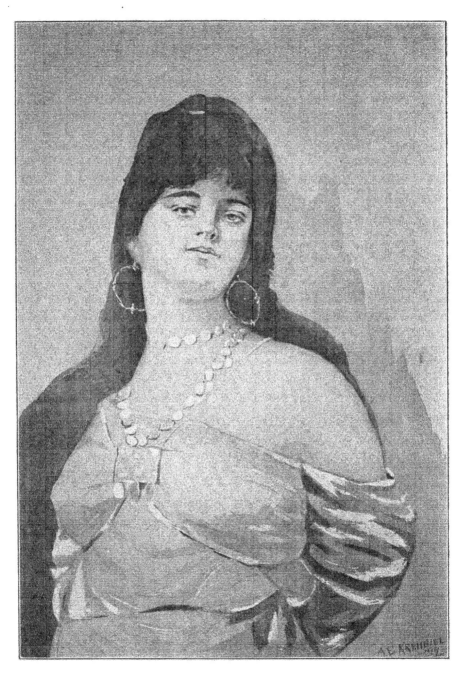

She was accredited the most beautiful woman in Mexico.
Page 26.

Juana La Garza. 27

Nacional, which should apprise her of his arrival to descend to the grand salon.

The furnishings of the boudoir, were just such as to form the ideal setting for a pretty woman. The floors were of glazed tiles, the tapestries red, with the upholstering of the furniture to match. A few rosewood settees, a large centre table of pietra dura, an iron bedstead with a great canopy, a dainty Venetian mirror, which reflected the beautiful image of the lady Juana la Garza, more times than one, during the day.

As the lady Juana la Garza dreamily watched the curling ring that rose in a haze of blue, from her cigarette, her face took on a gentler, softer look, as of a woman who dreams of the man she loves. Her lips half parted in a smile of sweet content, her eyes staring into the faraway of imagery,—it seemed as though an angel from on high had descended for the briefest space to earth, so beautiful was she.

Felicie the maid entered softly.

The lady half raised herself upon her arm.

" Ah—señora—how shall I tell you ? How shall I say it ? "

And the maid began to sob violently, rocking her form to and fro. The lady Juana la Garza sprang from the divan. Her brow contracted into a frown, her eyes assumed a steely glint of anger, her mouth hardened almost imperceptibly. She seized the girl roughly by the arm.

" Speak out, you fool, and stand not there

28   Iturbide, A Soldier of Mexico.

like one distraught. Come, tell me, what is it that frightens you?"

Still trembling, the affrighted maid muttered between her sobs.

"Alas, señora, we are lost, we are lost. Rafael Aristo has secured from the Viceroy your husband's pardon. He will be here to-night."

"To-night?—My husband will be here to-night?—Impossible," gasped the lady Juana la Garza, sinking again upon the divan, her face as colorless as marble, her form shaken by the violence of her passion, her lips quivering with anger unrestrained.

"I swear it by the Virgin,—it is the truth, señora. I had it from the priest, Rafael Aristo, who has but just come from the Government Palace," pursued the maid.

"Rafael Aristo—that devil," murmured the lady Juana la Garza softly to herself, and her eyes seemed to focus in a scintillating glitter of hate. "So the Head of the Society of Jesus betrays the Agent of the Society of Jesus. And it is this man who came between my husband and I, and broke up our home for the good of the Church of Rome. It is this man that transformed the innocent little convent maid into the woman of the world, that she might hold the Viceroy in the glamour of her fascination and guide the destinies of Mexico as the Church demanded. And now, this Head of the Society of Jesus has no more use for the woman whose life he ruined and

Juana La Garza. 29

takes this means of disposing of her, by setting free the dishonored husband whose home-coming means retribution." Then glancing at Felicie, the lady said aloud :—

"And Rafael Aristo—the priest—you say he is here ? "

" In the private passageway," responded the girl.

" Bid him come to me at once," imperiously continued her mistress; and her face again assumed a look of anguish she could not re-strain. The maid quickly left the room. The lady Juana la Garza buried her face in her hands.

" I am lost indeed," she sobbed ; " lost, lost, lost."

" Not lost, my daughter, not lost, for the Holy Church will save you," broke in the deep, musical voice of the Head of the Society of Jesus.

She looked up. Before her stood Rafael Aristo, a short, squat, smooth-shaven man, his face, sombre, sallow, forbidding,—his stumpy body inclined gently forward, and a great horny finger raised in warning to his thick lips while his great, glittering black, hypnotic eyes, fat encircled, rested significantly upon Felicie.

" Leave us, Felicie," said the lady Juana la Garza. The maid cast a look of intense dis-like upon the forbidding figure in gorgeous robes and mitre, and slowly, reluctantly left the room. The priest advanced nearer the

30   Iturbide, A Soldier of Mexico.

lady Juana la Garza and allowed his hypnotic eyes to rest for a long time upon her face until she trembled at the fiery intensity of the gaze and became once more the submissive daughter of the Church. Finally he spoke, and his voice was very soft and low :

"Courage, my daughter, courage," he said, " the Church guards its own. For the Church you left the arms of a husband who loved you to become the mistress of the Viceroy. The Church protected you then, and this trusting, accommodating husband was given over to the Inquisitors of the Church as a rebel. You are the only woman in Mexico who can sway these intriguing diplomats and hardened soldiers in the desperate game now playing. It is a life struggle between Church and State, between Royalist and Patriot, between the Society of Jesus and the Brotherhood of Freemasons. Three men have appeared upon the stage of Mexican politics—His Excellency the Viceroy, who to-day rules serenely over Mexico, by the grace of God and the favor of the Bourbons, the rebel General, Antonio Lopez de Santa Anna, who has at his back the Scottish Rite and the York Rite, the most powerful of the Masonic bodies in Mexico, and last our own Agustin de Iturbide, a great soldier but a young man of such boundless ambition that, while he is to-day for us, may be to-morrow against us. One of these three men must rule supreme. Two must fall. No secrets are hidden from the Society of Jesus. Our agents

Juana La Garza. 31

are everywhere. I know that Santa Anna is in hiding in the Capitol, that he ventured into this spider's web, for two things : the assassination of his great rival, Colonel Agustin de Iturbide and a night of love with the woman who is dearer to him than life itself, the lady Juana la Garza.

" What more fitting than the opportune return of a loving husband, to find the wife from whom he was rudely torn asunder, in the arms of the rebel General ? Think you not, my lady, his long months of imprisonment in the deepest dungeon of the Acordade, will not nerve his arm for vengeance ? Think you Santa Anna will ever leave your apartments alive ? "

" Ah, monster ! you have betrayed me," gasped the lady, sinking back half fainting upon the divan.

" I have saved you," calmly retorted the priest. " When General Santa Anna has been done to the death, I shall see to it that you are freed from the hated caresses of the Viceroy. Nay more, I will save you from your husband. Only play your part well. You alone know under what disguise the rebel General Santa Anna will pass the guards of the Viceroy. You alone can deliver to us this greatest enemy of the Church of Rome. Give him but one remotest word of warning that will enable him to escape us and I swear, as I am a true Churchman, that you shall suffer a fate worse than hell itself can give you. I have spoken and I think you understand."

32   Iturbide, A Soldier of Mexico.

"But I love him—my God! I love him!" sobbed the unhappy woman hoarsely. "And you ask me to lure him to his death."

"Bah!" retorted the priest with a vicious sneer, "you love him as you have loved other men—as once you loved your husband, the gallant Captain la Garza—as you once loved His Excellency—as you once loved Colonel Iturbide. Such love is the love of a woman who will pass into history as every man's wife."

"There spoke the Jesuit," sobbed the lady la Garza. "Teaching me in your convent that the end justified the means, deadening my young conscience by your poisonous sophistries, you have made a play of my beauty to lure to destruction the men who stood in the pathway of the Church of Rome. Oh, I am awearied of it all—I am awearied of it all. But I am not wholly bad nor as wicked as you would make me, and I refuse to betray the one man I have loved with a sincere affection—the only honest passion of my life—even for the Church of Rome, to which I gave all that any woman can give when I sacrificed mine honor."

The priest, Rafael Aristo, fixed upon her a stern, angry look and raised his arm impressively. But his voice was calm and he was in everything the priest—perfect in self-control.

"Listen, my lady, you do not know me yet. I have an old mother down in the provinces of the Southland—an old mother who lives for me alone and whose love is the one little ray of sunshine in all my life. And yet I tell you

Juana La Garza. 33

that if that dear old mother stood in the way of the Church of Rome, I'd crush her withered limbs upon the rack, and carry her broken body into the plaza to be burned with the heretics."

" Monster!" gasped the lady, her eyes dilated with an awful shuddering fear.

" I have raised you from a very little girl, my daughter. I have loved you as mine own, but I swear to you by the God above, that if you do not deliver to us this night the foul traitor who has fomented rebellion throughout the land, I myself will take you to a fate that is worse than any death of which you can dream."

The lady Juana la Garza looked long into the eyes of the priest Rafael Aristo and in them read the truth.

Rising with a beautiful resignation expressed upon her pallid features she murmured sadly :

" Tell me what you wish, my father, and I obey."

The priest raised his hand in benediction.

" There spoke the daughter of the Church," he said gently, with an oily, unctuous smile. " The rebel General, Antonio Lopez de Santa Anna, attends the masque ball in honor of the Viceroy this evening. It might be reasonable, you may say, to seize his person in the grand salon. But there will be friends in attendance upon him and extreme measures would lead to much bloodshed and precipitate a massacre, —perhaps cause a rising of the people. For Santa Anna is popular with the canaille. But

34 Iturbide, A Soldier of Mexico.

you can lure him here after the festivities and then when your husband comes to take vengeance, the world will cry " Well done," and the most dangerous enemy of the holy Church will have been quietly removed. And with Santa Anna and Iturbide dead, the Royalist power in Mexico, is secure, since the Viceroys are but puppets of the Church of Rome."

" I will this night give into your hands, General Santa Anna, the man I love," gasped the lady Juana la Garza and buried her face in her hands sobbing violently.

" Vengeance is mine, I will repay, saith the Lord." And the Head of the Society of Jesus raised his hand in benediction over her head.

" And now, my daughter, the blessing of the Church rest upon you, for you are about to show yourself a true daughter of the Church. To-night, a lover you lose, but greater than a lover your gain, the protection of the Church, the holy Church, the Church of Rome, more enduring than the world, all-powerful, perpetual, omnipresent, mighty Church. Love—life—time itself—must one and all give way before the onward march of the Church of Rome. I, Rafael Aristo, am the Church in Mexico, and being the Church have made you what you are,—to the world, a shameless wanton,—to me an instrument to lure the puppets of history to destruction for the good of what I represent, and I glory in my handi-work. Together we will rise up, you and I, up and up and up, over the racked bodies of

Juana La Garza. 35

our enemies, until there remains only one perpetual, all-existing thing—the Church—the
Church—the Church which in Mexico is I—I—
I—Rafael Aristo the priest, Rafael Aristo the
Jesuit, Rafael Aristo the future Richelieu of
the New World. Until, then, my daughter,
you are my very abject slave to work my will
upon these poor pitiable things that dare to
flaunt their mean ambitions in the face of the
will of the Holy Church. Until then, my
daughter, you are mine, mine, mine, all mine.
My will is your will. My ambition is your
ambition. Together we will rise up and up
and up, over the bleeding bodies of Santa
Anna and the rest, up perhaps even to a throne
—who knows?"

And Rafael Aristo, with the wild glare of
the fanatic in his lurid, gleaming, snake-like
eyes, looked sternly upon the little lady who,
crushed, fascinated, hypnotized, had risen and
stood trembling before him.

From the grand salon came the martial
notes of the Palace band sounding the overture
to the Hymno Nacional, and the priest extended his hand to the lady Juana la Garza.

"His Excellency has come at last," he said
softly. "Come, my daughter, let us join the
merrymakers."

Still trembling she allowed him to lead her
down the grand stairway and into the presence
of His Excellency, Don Juan Apodaca, Viceroy of Mexico, by the grace of God and the
favor of the Bourbons.

36 Iturbide, A Soldier of Mexico.

CHAPTER III.

A MASON AT SIGHT.

AT Dahalia's affrighted, anguished cry, Colonel Iturbide turned quickly and saw a tall slender gentleman, in ultra clerical black, with a great sugar-loafed hat, beneath which were features pale, handsome and regular,—eyes large and dreamy,—and a brow lofty and intellectual, albeit half hidden by a cluster of jet-black curls.

"General Don Antonio Lopez de Santa Anna," he muttered in deep astonishment.

"Or for the present, Padre Ybanez, Lord Bishop of Vera Cruz," replied the rebel General in a soft, musical voice.

And gently supporting Dahalia, who had recovered from her momentary weakness, Santa Anna continued :

"A few moments ago, I had it in my mind to deprive the Viceroy of his most trusted councillor and Spain of her most intrepid commander."

And he displayed beneath a fold of his cassock, a long, murderous-looking stiletto.

"'Twould have been an easy matter, señor Colonel," he continued, with a short, rasping laugh. "But curiosity stayed my hand and

A Mason at Sight. 37

saved a new leader for the National forces, at present termed rebels. And so señor, first of the Mexicans, I greet you as future Liberator of our country."

And he made a graceful bow to which Iturbide responded with a warm embrace. For Iturbide remembered that this man was the brother of the woman he loved.

"You are mad, Antonio," gasped Dahalia, her cheek paling at thought of her brother's peril. "Know you not that there is a price upon your head as one of the proscribed? That you can expect no mercy from the Viceroy, for His Excellency is cruel and heartless and would gladly give you over to the tortures of the Inquisitors. Ah, my God, my brother, you have come voluntarily to your death——"

"Not to my death, little sister, but to the arms of the woman I love," replied Santa Anna carelessly. "To the arms of the lady Juana la Garza, who is even now awaiting me in her salon."

"Juana la Garza—ah, Dios,—you love that terrible woman?" sobbed the girl. "You are going to meet the creature whose heart is blacker than the night about us, who has toyed with the affections of good men and true, only to betray them when she is awearied, or if she permits them to escape her toils at last sends them forth broken, ruined, dishonored gentlemen. You are going to the woman who betrayed me to the Viceroy, and sent me out into the streets alone and friendless because I

38   Iturbide, A Soldier of Mexico.

would not close my eyes to her wickedness,—because I saved one man at least—the future Liberator of our country—from her wiles and fascinations?   Ah, my brother, tell me you do not love her—tell me you do not love her."

"I cannot," murmured Santa Anna. "For she is my all—my life, my Mexico, my world. When we of the Southland love, my sister, it is an all-consuming passion, and so with me, my whole future is in the hands of this woman. If my love for her should lead me to the very gates of hell, cheerfully would I go on and on and on.   Of her past I know nothing and care less.   I only know that I love her and loving her I would die for her.   Patriot and all that I am, I would betray my dear Mexico if need be for the love of Juana la Garza, the fairest, sweetest, dearest lady in all the land.   So it is useless to plead with me.   I came here to-night at the risk of my life to carry out the mission unfulfilled and kill the man who has led the victorious armies of old Spain over the bodies of my countrymen.   But a merciful Providence intervened to save from assassination the most intrepid soldier our country has produced. And so, chiquita,—to-night for me will be a night of love.   To-morrow—the camp again, and battle and bloodshed.   To-night a night of idle dalliance with the sweetest lady in all the world to me.   To-morrow——"

"To-morrow, Antonio,—ah, Santo Dios, I shudder at thought of what the morrow may have in store!" sobbed Dahalia.

A Mason at Sight. 39

Santa Anna turned abruptly to Colonel Iturbide and grasped his hand warmly.

"Amigo mio, to-night I sought your life and found your friendship. Until a short while ago I feared you and, fearing you, came here to kill you. Now, trusting you I confide to you the honor of my little sister, Dahalia. She is all I have, señor, and if aught should befall her I believe it would break my heart. It has been said of you, Colonel Iturbide, that you are the most gallant of all the gentlemen in Mexico, and I know that you will guard the honor of the sister of Santa Anna as you would guard your own."

"As I would guard my own," said the Royalist Colonel, raising his hand solemnly.

"I am a marked man, the country through," continued Santa Anna. "About to venture my all for the sake of the woman I love, I look to you, my new found friend and brother-in-arms, to see that my sister has safe conduct from the Capitol. Due west from the city, some few leagues is a little wayside meson, the Posada del Sabinal, where at present are the most trusted of my officers. They await the coming of a million-dollar convoy of the Viceroy."

"Dios—a million-dollar convoy!" gasped Iturbide, his pale face flushed with interest and excitement. "The General who is able to intercept that convoy will have Mexico at his feet."

"And Mexico is the stake for which we are

40 Iturbide, A Soldier of Mexico.

playing," pursued Santa Anna calmly. "With the convoy of the Viceroy in our hands, we can levy troops sufficient to drive the Spanish forces south to the sea. My duty told me to stay and possess myself of the wealth that would make me master of Mexico. My love summoned me to the side of the lady Juana la Garza. And so my friend, I turn over the command of the National forces to you."

"And my warrant?" asked Iturbide, the light of a great ambition shining in his eyes.

" The signet ring of Santa Anna," replied his companion, passing a heavy seal to the Royalist Colonel. " It is the sign of the thirty-third degree. The wearer of that ring can move at will the mysterious brotherhood of Mexican Freemasons. With that seal you can rally to your standard the forces of Guerrero, Guadalupe Victoria, and those other patriot chiefs who have carried on the struggle begun by Hidalgo long years ago. And first of the Mexicans, I make you a Mason at sight by virtue of my power as head of the Scottish Rite. You are one, for and with us, now and for all time, in life and in eternity."

Reverently the Royalist Colonel kissed the great seal of the rebel General Santa Anna, and for a few moments the two conversed apart from Dahalia. Then Santa Anna, embracing his sister, turned and with a gentle " Adios," vanished into the darkness of the night.

The Fête in Honor of the Viceroy. 41

CHAPTER IV.

THE FÊTE IN HONOR OF THE VICEROY.

ALONG the whole length of the Calle de San Francisco, there was a great crush of aristocratic equipages with a rich blazoning of armorial escutcheons and emblems of rank. At the entrance of the Casa Garza, a company of chasseurs, in full-dress uniforms, were drawn up four deep.

In the grand salon of the Casa Garza, the scene was one of ever-varying pageantry and splendor. Pretty Poblana girls, in merino dresses of bright hues, bespangled and gold bedecked,—serious looking Contadinas in white, —grave nuns and novices, elbowed with fierce-looking soldiers of the time, serious-visaged Jesuits, gloomy Trappists, Mestizos and reincarnated Viceroys.

There were La Vallières, Nell Gwynns, and Montespans. For each there was a Royal Louis and a Charles.

From the richly garnished boxes with their Chinese lanterns, the staid and portly lady patronesses with their muchly bepowdered faces, their lavish diamonds and great coiffures looked down upon the merrymakers.

The select band of the "Viceroy's Own"

42   Iturbide, A Soldier of Mexico.

furnished the orchestral accompaniment to the dancing.

Under one of the lamps, in a secluded portion of the grand salon, a Padre in a violet robe, scarlet cloak, and shovel hat, was conversing in a whisper with an Inquisitor in black.

The Padre was the General, Don Antonio Lopez de Santa Anna.

The Inquisitor was His Excellency, the Viceroy of Mexico, by the Grace of God and the favor of the Bourbons.

"And so, my Lord Bishop of Vera Cruz, you will have it that this Santa Anna is not so bad as he has been painted?" laughed His Excellency, slapping his companion upon the back.

"In faith, Your Excellency," replied Santa Anna in equally jocular vein responding to the other's mood, "in faith, Your Excellency, Santa Anna and I were boys together—buen companeros, and in my opinion, no better fellow lives than he who has, through the misinterpretation of his enemies, been maligned and termed a bandit."

"A fine fellow indeed," sneered the Viceroy, "levying tribute on His Sovereign Majesty the King, pillaging the clergy, burning villages and planning raids upon our soldiery. 'Twas only two months back, my Lord Bishop, that we were told how Santa Anna and his band invaded the sacred precincts of your Palace and made Your Reverence and your suite to stand upon your heads like a lot of mummers, while they feasted at your table."

The Fête in Honor of the Viceroy. 43

"A merry jest in truth," replied his companion. "A jest which I forgive Santa Anna, because of our old comradeship."

"But a jest which we will not forgive nor forget," replied the Viceroy. "Listen, Lord Bishop of Vera Cruz. I have set a price upon the rascal's head. If he be taken alive it will be more to my liking."

"And why, Your Excellency?" asked Santa Anna with one of those penetrating glances which marked the man.

"That I may amuse myself," hissed the Viceroy, a vindictive look of hate mantling his bilious face. "We take not so many rebels, even in these troublous times, that the Inquisition palls upon us. For myself, I can conceive no happier moment than when the Inquisitor puts the question to some poor devil of a patriot self-styled. The groans and cries, the blood-stained rack, the stoicism with which so many meet the question are all music to mine ears. I sometimes feel a touch of pity and admiration when some poor fool yields up his last gasp for the imaginary ideal he calls his country. And I have heard so much of this guerilla chieftain, that I am assured he would afford a most amusing spectacle upon the rack."

"A spectacle I fear you will not soon see, Excellency," replied Santa Anna tersely.

"Eh—what—and why—?" asked the Viceroy abruptly, casting a half suspicious glance upon his companion.

"Quien sabe? Excellency," replied Santa

44   Iturbide, A Soldier of Mexico.

Anna with a careless shrug of his shoulders. "Only I have heard it said that Santa Anna has sworn never to be taken alive. Too well he knows the cruelty of our Viceroys, a matter of history. 'Twas only a short time back, Excellency, when he saw a former Captain of the Royal forces, noted for his great strength and manly beauty, torn from his home and delivered over to the Inquisitors. Once again he saw that man—a broken reed, gray-haired at twenty-five, weak and decrepit, yet sustained by one great, all-consuming desire—vengeance. And that man will return to his dishonored home to-night."

The Viceroy started.

Then with a cruel, hard laugh.

"His name, señor, tell me his name that I may prepare a fit reception."

For the Viceroy had no thought of Captain la Garza whose wife he delighted to honor.

"His name—his name——" echoed Santa Anna. Then suddenly:

"Ah pardon, Excellency—one moment—our hostess does me the honor to invite me to her box."

And with a gallant bow he hastened towards the box of the lady Juana la Garza leaving the astonished Viceroy staring after him.

As he knelt before the most beautiful woman in Mexico, Santa Anna could only look and look and look.

Such beauty as hers made him speechless.

With a graceful genuflexion, the lady Juana

The Fête in Honor of the Viceroy. 45

la Garza, inclined gently towards him, and in a voice that trembled, in spite of her apparent composure, whispered:

"Antonio, you must leave this house at once—for its very atmosphere is death-exhaling. In five minutes it will be too late—perhaps is even now too late."

"But your promise?" whispered Santa Anna. "Is this my reward for neglecting my duty and periling my life, to once more enclasp you in my arms? Ah, Juana,—heart of my heart—dear one, you no longer love me."

"It is because I love you that I bid you go, Antonio," murmured the lady, trembling with passion and the glow of the lovelight in her eyes.

"The real Bishop of Vera Cruz, whose robes you wear, has escaped from your lines and is even now in the anteroom awaiting a private audience with the Viceroy."

"Carramba! This is indeed serious," muttered Santa Anna. Then with a sudden resolution:

"I will not go, I can outface the Bishop of Vera Cruz and denounce him before the Viceroy as an impostor."

"It will not avail," said the lady la Garza. "And even so, this danger passed, there is another to be met. My husband returns to-night —for vengeance—and for me."

"I knew it," said Santa Anna. "And I came here to take you with me to the National Camp. Ah, Juana, come with me to-night and

46   Iturbide, A Soldier of Mexico.

I will defend you in my hacienda of Mango de Clavo, though all the picked forces of the Viceroy are sent against me.   Come—my darling—Juana."

"To-night—impossible!" gasped the lady la Garza. "This house is closely watched by the Inquisitors of the Church of Rome, and if I should attempt to leave the salon with you, it would mean death—your death and mine."

"Ah Dios, my darling, let us die together then, since we cannot live together," cried Santa Anna recklessly.

"No, Antonio, we will live for the future," replied the lady. "Listen, my love. Do you escape this nest of our enemies to-night and I swear to you that on the morrow, I will join you at Mango de Clavo."

"You swear that, Juana? You swear that?" cried Santa Anna joyfully, and would have seized her in a fond embrace, forgetting all else save his love, had she not waved him gently back.

"I swear it by my mother's memory." she murmured.

"Then *hasta la vista*, my darling—till we meet again," said Santa Anna and pressing his lips gently upon her little hand, he mingled with the crowd of merrymakers, passed to the grand staircase and calmly brushed by the guard at the portals of the Casa Garza.

When he had disappeared from view, the lady Juana la Garza pressed her hand to her side and sank upon the divan.

The Fête in Honor of the Viceroy. 47

"My lover is saved, but I—I am lost beyond hope," she gasped. "For that accursed priest said that if I did not this night deliver Santa Anna to his enemies, he himself would take me to a fate far worse than any death of which I could dream. Well, it is better so. By this one word of warning, I make atonement for my wretched past and save for Mexico her great patriot leader. And when General Antonio Lopez de Santa Anna has marched triumphant into the Capitol, driving his enemies before him, when he has raised the red, white and green banner of Independence over the Palace of the Viceroys perhaps then he'll think sometimes of the wretched woman to whom he first recalled the sense of womanhood and her duty to her country, the woman who to-night has betrayed the Society of Jesus to the Brotherhood of Freemasons, because she loves Santa Anna."

"Juana, you are not yourself,—you are sad —you weep."

It was the effeminate lisp of His Excellency, Don Juan Apodaca, Viceroy of Mexico.

The lady Juana la Garza looked at Don Juan Apodaca as he stood under the glare of many lights, bowing low and smiling with the self-assurance of one of absolute power and her face took on an expression of icy reserve that was almost contempt. And this insignificant, dissipated, aristocratic little Manling with his smooth-shaven, pallid face, his scarlet and gold uniform just showing under his cassock, this

48   Iturbide, A Soldier of Mexico.

man had come between husband and wife and made her a wanton?

Dios—how she hated the man.

"I have come to bid you farewell, Juana. For I go to a private audience with the Captain of the City Guard and the Lord Bishop of Vera Cruz," continued the Viceroy.

She started. The Lord Bishop of Vera Cruz! If the Viceroy should see him and learn of Santa Anna's deception, he would set on foot all the vast machinery of the soldiery, and throw such a cordon of troops around the city, that the rebel General must eventually be captured. No, the Viceroy must not be permitted to attend this audience.

The lady Juana la Garza became at once the fascinating, beautiful woman of the world.

With her most charming smile, she took the Viceroy's hand, gently in her own.

"Your Excellency shows me but scant courtesy," she murmured softly. "I have so looked forward to the moment when you would spend another night at Casa Garza and whisper in my ears the old familiar story. But no—your love for me is on the wane. You are like all the rest, and I had learned to think your love, at least, something more than the fleeting pastime of a moment."

"Valgame Dios—Juana— my darling—you love me still, and I—poor wretched fool—I thought you had long since wearied of your Viceroy."

The Fête in Honor of the Viceroy. 49

And His Excellency dropping upon his knees seized her little hand rapturously.

Nor did she withdraw it.

"Your Excellency will ever be my foremost thought in life," she said, smiling upon him. "Since you and you alone awakened in my soul first thought of love, I forgive your recent neglect, but conditionally."

"Conditionally?" echoed the Viceroy.

"Come with me to my boudoir and suffer the tiresome old Bishop of Vera Cruz to cool his heels in the anteroom until morning. It will do him good."

"But the matter is of moment—there are strange rumors ——" began the Viceroy.

"Ah, you hesitate between a prosaic old priest and a night of love?" broke in the lady poutingly.

"Dios no!" replied the Viceroy. "Else would I not be a man! so, lead on, señora, to the boudoir."

"And to my husband, libertine," whispered the lady as she smilingly took his arm.

50 Iturbide, A Soldier of Mexico.

CHAPTER V.

THE MILLION–DOLLAR CONVOY OF THE VICEROY.

AT every exit from the Capitol, a cordon of the City Guard performed sentry duty, with instructions to allow no one to pass their lines without the password.

The password had been changed by the Viceroy at the hour of the Angelus.

A little band of scarlet troopers, the most devoted and intrepid of Colonel Iturbide's regiment—men who would have followed him to the very gates of Hell—awaited only a word from their beloved leader to make a dash for liberty.

But Iturbide remembered that the woman he loved rode at his side, and he would not needlessly endanger her life by a sudden dash through the Royalist lines.

" A hundred and twenty of us, amigos," he said. " Now do you, Captain Lara, assume command of this troop and I will see the officer of the guard, and if possible persuade him to pass my men. If not we must cut our way through. This lady rides in the center of the troop and I hold each one of you re-

The Million-Dollar Convoy.   51

sponsible for her safety.   You understand, my friends?"

The troopers saluted, and Captain Lara placed himself at the head of the column.

Iturbide approached the sentry, who, recognizing his Colonel's insignia, in the glare of the flambeaux, saluted.   In a brusque voice the Colonel cried:

"The Acapulco troop of Los Rojos—one hundred and twenty strong."

The officer of the City Guard saluted.

"And the password, señor Colonel?"

"Is it necessary in my case, amigo?" blandly asked Iturbide.

"My orders, señor Colonel."

"And you cannot pass my troop upon my recognizance?" pursued Iturbide.

"Impossible, señor Colonel.   My orders were most strict," said the man.

"Have you tablets with you?" asked Iturbide.

The man nodded and handed them to his interlocutor.

Iturbide hastily wrote upon them,

"Ultima ratio regum—Iturbide."

That is to say—War!

And handing them to the man added, "For the Viceroy."

Then raising his saber above his head Iturbide cried:

"Attention—soldiers of the Reds!"

The troopers straightened themselves in their saddles.

52 Iturbide, A Soldier of Mexico.

"And the password, señor Colonel?" persisted the sentry, this time grasping the bridle of Iturbide's horse.

"Is this," replied Iturbide, striking the fellow between the eyes with the hilt of his sword. The sentry fell to the ground moaning. There was an instant commotion in the camp of the City Guard, and a running to arms.

"Forward!" cried Iturbide waving his sword.

And the scarlet-clad troop dashed through the camp, riding down many a poor devil who chanced to be in their path.

The pace was kept up for several leagues and then lessened to an ordinary cavalry trot. There seemed to be an unusually large crowd of pilgrims, canonigos, and leperos traveling the road towards the Capitol, and Captain Lara, smiling, grimly said:

"We are safe from pursuit, Colonel mine."

"And I on the contrary think we will be hard put to it," said Iturbide meditatively.

"Noticed you the pilgrims and leperos on the road behind us, Colonel mine?" asked Captain Lara.

"A somewhat out of-the-ordinary number of wayfarers," was the reply.

"They are the outposts of the rebel forces," continued Captain Lara. "And, por Dios, the whole cordon of the City Guard could not pass them by in time to overtake us."

"Then press we on to the Posada del Sabinal," said Iturbide. "If we overhaul the

The Million Dollar Convoy. 53

million-dollar convoy of the Viceroy, we sound the death knell of Spanish rule in Mexico."

The night was well on. A gibbous moon threw weird, ghastly shadows into the guest-room of the Posada del Sabinal, where at a long table, four priests and a stylishly dressed woman in a rich riding habit of green and gold, sat over their wine conversing in whispers.

A slatternly, wheezing old boniface, limped around a little more rapidly than was his wont, because the Blessed Virgin, did not usually favor him with such a large patronage—and so select—four priests and a lady. And the landlord of the Posada del Sabinal, in the intervals of leisure offered him, wheezed out a few extra prayers to the Blessed Virgin and told off a few additional beads on his rosary. For the landlord's heart was glad.

Presently, the lady left her companions, and going to the open door shaded her eyes in the most vain endeavor to discern if there might be any wayfarers or soldiery approaching along the endless, dry, alkali, dusty road.

Before her stretched a vast tableland, sparse of vegetation, save for the great organ cacti, sending their giant stalks in every direction. and the less conspicuous chaparral and mesquit bushes through which the sinuous, winding road curled in and out, losing itself in the distance. To the east not a sign of human being or animal. To the west the road wound abruptly off from the Posada del Sabinal, hidden by the abnormally large cacti, ever increas-

54   Iturbide, A Soldier of Mexico.

ing in size as they were nearer the bare mountains and higher altitude.

About a mile above the inn, in the desert, a
road from the south intersected the main road.
This the young woman could not see from her
coigne of observation.   But her sense of hearing trained to a superfine acuteness, caught the
faintest rumble of the wheels in the distance.

" The convoy of the Viceroy," she cried,
turning quickly to her companions.

" Confusion to the Viceroy," said the priests
rising and clutching their glasses.

The young woman abruptly closed the door,
fastening the latch on the inside.

" Courage—companeros ! "   she murmured,
resuming her place at the head of the table.

And now the heavy rumble of the conducta,
along the hard, dry road, was heard, broken by
the cracking of whips and the hoarse cries of
the escort.

There was the sound of horsemen without,
followed by a loud knocking and a few choice
oaths.

" Oiga—Santo Dios—open in the name of the
Viceroy ! " growled a harsh, rough voice.

" Coming—brave señores—coming," wheezed
the old boniface, limping to the door and loos-
ing the latch.

" Well—Mother of God—it is time—" quoth
the newcomer, very angrily, stalking into the
room.

Then seeing the lady he made an awkward
military bow, his helmet in his hand, saying :

The Million-Dollar Convoy. 55

"Your pardon, señora, and fathers all."

"Granted, Captain mine, right readily, if you will join us at table," said the lady graciously.

"That I may not do, señorita," returned the stranger; "but I will gladly join you in a copita of wine. And then I must push on, by order of His Excellency."

"And suppose I should give you His Excellency's permission to tarry with us here?" asked the lady with a winning smile.

"And were it possible, I would too gladly stay," rejoined the stranger, "for the night promises to be a stormy one."

"Then, señor Capitan, know that I am the Viceroy's niece, Señora Fernandez, sent here to intercept your conducta," said the lady and smiled upon him.

"To intercept the conducta—?" faltered the officer. "Then you know——?"

"I know, señor Capitan, that a million-dollar convoy, with but one troop of cavalry, even though they be of our 'Viceroy's Own,' cannot with safety risk the roads these troublous times. And so I asked my uncle to forward an additional force for your protection."

"Most kind and considerate lady, I thank you," responded the officer; "but I think, nevertheless, your fears are groundless. No sign of human being have we met upon the road this day."

"And yet they say that Santa Anna and his dare-devils are abroad," replied the lady.

56   Iturbide, A Soldier of Mexico.

" Bah—a mere boy," contemptuously replied the officer.

" And Guerrero and his guerillas," added the lady.

"An old man," replied the officer. "I would despatch them both at short notice with their canaille—for they could make no organized resistance to the picked troops of the Viceroy's Own. Still, to please the mood of one so fair, I will wait the coming of the reinforcements."

And excusing himself, the Captain went out to direct the corralling of the convoy.

The priests and the lady indulged in no little merriment at the expense of the unsuspecting officer.

The future of Mexico rests in the possession of this convoy," muttered one of the priests, looking thoughtfully into the carafe of sparkling wine before him.

" Dios—with a million in bullion—almost any man might precipitate a revolution," added the lady, then paused abruptly.

The strange officer had returned.

"Pardon the delay, lady," he said. " And now to introduce myself—Captain Berdejo of the Jalapa troop of the Viceroy's Own."

" And my father confessor, Fray Jimenez, de profession Catolico, Apostolico y Romano," replied the lady indicating the tall priest at her left with a graceful gesture.

The two men shook hands and embraced, and then the tall priest introduced his companions.

The Million-Dollar Convoy. 57

The Captain of the Convoy took his seat at the lady's right and gallantly accepted the copita of wine which she offered him.

Then ensued a brilliant and spirited conversation, interspersed with many a jest and story.

Two hours passed.

A terrific peal of thunder, followed by a blinding flash of lightning, for a moment silenced the party.

Outside the wind was howling with a fierce and angry gusto, and such a downpour of heavy rain was falling as falls in Mexico alone.

"Drink up, drink up, señor Captain, and thank the good God that you have a friendly shelter overhead on this night of all nights," laughed the lady, desirous of keeping the officer's attention from without."

"I do indeed thank the good God," replied Captain Berdejo crossing himself. "But I could have sworn I heard the clash of sabers and the shouting of voices in combat."

"Nonsense, amigo—the storm has unmanned you," softly purred the lady with a merriment she did not feel, for she, too, fancied she heard the clash of steel upon steel.

A sonorous crash from the heavens above almost drowned her voice, and the rain fell with increasing vigor.

"My lady there is nothing terrifying to Captain Berdejo, of the Viceroy's Own," said the officer gravely. "And His Excellency well knew that his convoy, entrusted to my troop, was absolutely safe."

58   Iturbide, A Soldier of Mexico.

" Even from Santa Anna ? " asked the lady.

" Aye, from Santa Anna—from Guerrero—from Guadalupe Victoria——"

The door opened and a great gust of wind extinguished the flickering candles. A vivid peal followed by another. Then a tense flash of lightning showed the startled merrymakers the figure of a man in the uniform of the Blues, bleeding from many wounds and leaning upon a reddened saber.

And then darkness.

But in a break of the storm, a faint, ever weakening voice, the voice of a dying man, growing ever fainter and fainter.

" Mother of God—we fought—Captain—but the Reds—Iturbide—ah Dios——"

The sound of a dull thud and the clang of steel against the wall.

Then silence.

All were upon their feet, awed by this apparition of the night. One of the priests lit a candle.

Captain Berdejo was leaning back against the wall like one distraught, whose faculties had taken sudden leave.

" What—what—does the man mean ? " he asked faintly.

" He means that you have been the guest of Santa Anna's sister, señor Captain," said the young woman. " He means that the convoy of His Excellency will never reach the Capitol."

" You—you—ah, she-devil ! " shrieked Captain Berdejo, frantically grasping his sword hilt.

The Million-Dollar Convoy. 59

But the lady pressed the point of a jeweled stiletto to his throat and calmly looking into his face said :

" Patience, my brave Captain. Your cause is irrevocably lost."

And the Captain of the Convoy could only look into that pretty, laughing face, for he read death in the limpid black eyes.

By the flickering candlelight, he could see the black, statue-like forms of the priests standing immobile in their places—a silent dead thing in a tattered, blood-bespattered blue uniform, lying disordered in the doorway, —the slim figure of a young girl in a riding habit, calmly pressing her murderous stiletto upon his throat.

Simultaneously the room was filled with a crowd of blood-bespattered troopers, in scarlet uniforms, with great shakos and encrimsoned sabers.

One man separated himself from his fellows, one man in the gold and scarlet uniform of a Colonel of cavalry, and advanced towards the tall priest with the light of battle still shining in his eyes.

Troopers and priests fell upon their knees with the exception of the tall man in black, the sister of Santa Anna, and Captain Berdejo who leaned weakly against the wall.

" The million-dollar convoy of the Viceroy is ours and Mexico has found her master at last," cried Iturbide triumphantly.

And Dahalia, as she looked upon him, stand-

60   Iturbide, A Soldier of Mexico.

ing there could not but compare him with the inferior men of his suite.

He was more like a European or an American than a Mexican. Five feet nine in height, of muscular build, possessing markedly oval features, a complexion of a peculiar whitish pallor, and brown hair and side whiskers, he offered a striking contrast to the swarthy faced men who surrounded him.

And as she looked, came into her eyes the glow of the lovelight, and gently clasping his hand she murmured:

"My hero—my Emperor—my love."

CHAPTER VI.

THE BEDCHAMBER OF JUANA LA GARZA.

THE faintest streak of dawn was just breaking over the Capitol. In the distance, through the dim light of early morning, loomed up the white-capped peaks of Popocatapetl and Iztaccihuatl. Beautiful indeed they looked in the shimmer of the early dawn.

Across the courtyard of the Casa Garza, two men moved noiselessly,—a priest in a black cassock, and a soldier in a worn blue uniform, wearing the insignia of a Captain of the " Viceroy's Own." In a darkened corner of the courtyard, well hidden under the shadow of the palace, a troop of helmeted hussars were drawn up at attention, awaiting the order of their officer.

The two men entered a private passage-way and as noiselessly ascended to the salon above.

" You desire to meet this man alone ? " asked the priest doubtfully.

" Alone? Ah Dios, yes," rejoined the officer in a subdued voice tremulous with passion. " After all, your reverence, he is only a man and I would be but a poor husband if I could not defend mine honor. Wait you here until I have returned and if I do not return within ten minutes you may know that I have

62   Iturbide, A Soldier of Mexico.

fallen and sound the alarm to the troopers that this foul libertine may never leave Casa Garza alive."

And he left the priest a solitary, anxious figure at the door.

The lady Juana la Garza, stole silently from the great canopied bed, and moved gently to the window, a sad-faced, pitiful looking, little figure in white.   Her beautiful, wavy hair, fell in great curls, over her waxen shoulders.   The open folds of her robe de nuit, revealed a magnificent bosom, that rose and fell in rapid pulsations, in consonance with her breathing.

The Viceroy slept.

The lady la Garza lighted a candle from the braziero.

Then paused, her lips half parted in a sort of nameless terror, her eyes dilated with a sudden fear.

For at the door opening into the salon, she distinctly heard a low, steady knocking.

"Ah God—my husband——" she murmured faintly, " have I the courage to look him in the face?   And after all that he has suffered because of his love for me?   It is my punishment and I will make my atonement to the man whose name I bear and whose name I have dishonored."

With trembling hands the lady Juana la Garza flung wide the door and looked at the wretched man, who stood there, silent, grim and sorrowful, in his tattered blue uniform, still dank with the musty odors of a prison cell.

The Lady Juana la Garza flung wide the door and looked at the wretched man who stood there, silent, grim and sorrowful.

Page 62.

The Bedchamber of Juana La Garza. 63

For a moment they did not move.

Then the lady Juana la Garza, like one in a dream, moved slowly back, her eyes fixed with an awful fascination upon this broken old young man, whom she had last seen in all the splendor of glorious young manhood.

He had not drawn his sword.

With no weapon but the light of righteous indignation, and outraged honor in his eyes, he followed her silently into the boudoir.

And he too looked with an awful fascination upon the beautiful woman, who cowered there before him.

She seemed almost too young to die.

He felt sorry for her.

He felt sorry for himself.

Perhaps he had better go away and leave this woman to her sin.

Perhaps——

A deep sigh from the sleeping Viceroy recalled him to a sense of his duty.

He stepped over to the window and drew aside the curtain, allowing the glorious sun rays to stream full into the apartment.

The Viceroy stirred restlessly in his slumber.

Captain la Garza drew aside the canopy of the bed, and stood there looking at the sleeping man, his eyes fixed, hypnotic, intent,—his arms folded upon his breast.

The lady Juana la Garza, had fallen upon her knees and was telling her rosary, before a little altar near the window.

64   Iturbide, A Soldier of Mexico.

Gradually the Viceroy stirred restlessly—yawned—opened his eyes,—and encountered the stern, unrelenting gaze of Capitan la Garza.

"Diable!—betrayed, by heaven!" he exclaimed, raising himself to a sitting posture.

Then as Capitan la Garza made no movement, the Viceroy continued:

"I suppose it is an assassination. Well, then, strike, señor. I am ready."

And he bared his breast.

Captain la Garza, contemptuously pointed to the Viceroy's sword which lay upon a chair with his clothes.

"It is not an assassination, Excellency. It is retribution. Draw and defend yourself, before I forget that I am a gentleman of Mexico and strike an unarmed man."

His tones were hard and merciless.

The Viceroy sprang from the bed and throwing a dressing-gown loosely over his shoulders, drew his sword with trembling hand.

Very leisurely Captain la Garza divested himself of his coat and rolled up his sleeves, and in turn drew his saber.

The two men saluted and Captain la Garza advanced upon the Viceroy.

Their blades crossed.

Then indeed there was pretty swordplay. The duello was one between skilled swordsmen. It was advance and retreat, lunge, parry, parade and riposte, to the metallic rasping of the steel.

Slowly La Garza drove the Viceroy back, for

The Bedchamber of Juana La Garza. 65

he had it in his mind to pin him against the wall.

His Excellency made a furious lunge and the point of his sword just missed his opponent's heart. His Excellency gave vent to a savage cry of joy, as a small red spot appeared upon La Garza's shirt-front.

But the Captain, all oblivious to his wound, pressed his enemy the more closely.

Sparks of fire played along the two blades.

And La Garza's blade snapped asunder.

" I have you," shouted the Viceroy.

" Not yet," hissed la Garza.

And parrying the Viceroy's furious thrust, with his broken blade, he seized him by the throat and forced him back against the wall his sinewy hands encircling His Excellency as in a vise,—one, long, slender, snakelike, creeping around the Viceroy's throat,—the other grasping the Viceroy's right hand, pinning it with the sword, hard upon the wall behind.

The Viceroy gagged and choked. That awful, anaconda-like clasp, tightened around his throat, strangling him, killing him. That awful, placid face, with the great, black eyes, peering into his with a ghastly smile—the face of Captain la Garza—ah, Dios,—he would carry it to the grave———. This must be death, indeed.

Through his fast glazing eyes he became aware of a newcomer in the room.

The priest, Rafael Aristo.

And the Viceroy fainted.

5

66 Iturbide, A Soldier of Mexico.

When His Excellency gradually recovered consciousness, he became aware of many martial, uniformed officers surrounding him where he lay upon the bed,—of a pale, disheveled woman, sobbing near the window,—of the priest, Rafael Aristo.

And of the still, silent figure of Captain la Garza, lying full length upon the floor, a great gash upon his head.

" Madre de Dios, Your Excellency—the good God sent me here in time to save you," cried the priest joyfully. " A moment more and it would have been too late—too late."

The Viceroy rose slowly and walked over to the prostrate body of Captain la Garza. He looked down upon it for a long time and spurned it with his foot. Then turned away.

" Is the man dead ? " he asked finally.

One of the officers knelt over the prostrate figure and placed his ear to the chest.

" His heart still beats faintly, Excellency," he said.

" Bueno," muttered the Viceroy grimly. Then pointing to the sobbing woman, he continued :

" Holy father, I came between this woman and this man, in the long ago. I unite them again. The woman would have betrayed me. The man has dared to raise his hand against God's anointed. See to it that they spend their second honeymoon in the deepest dungeon of the Fortress of San Juan de Uloa."

The Bedchamber of Juana La Garza. 67

The lady Juana la Garza, uttered a fearful cry of terror and agony.

"Ah, Your Excellency, mercy, mercy," she sobbed. "I swear as God is my judge, I am innocent."

The priest, Rafael Aristo, roughly seized her slender wrists, and bending over until his hot, fevered breath touched her cheek, he hissed:

"Silence, woman. I promised you a fate far, far worse than death if you failed us. Daughter of the Church, no longer,—come to the dungeons of San Juan de Uloa,—the beginning of the end."

And he would have dragged her to her feet, but that with a final shriek—

"The dungeons of San Juan de Uloa—hell upon earth,—ah God——"

She fainted.

68   Iturbide, A Soldier of Mexico.

CHAPTER VII.

THE HONOR OF SANTA ANNA.

His Excellency the Viceroy of Mexico sat at table, surrounded by the officers of his staff. The cuisine was of the richest, and the wines were of the best. But there was no laughter upon the Viceroy's face.

The furnishings of the apartment were of the most luxurious. Satin upholstery, rugs of the richest furs, massive old plate with the Vice-regal crest, old-world china, great rosewood chairs of state, and satin-draped settees, gave an air of almost regal magnificence to the sur-roundings.

His Excellency was holding one of his famous councils in dressing-gown and slippers, but even so his costume was of the most elegant.

The Viceroy then did not laugh, for there were many vacant chairs at this informal coun-cil of war. At such a crisis when a simple up-rising had developed into a revolution, when the victorious armies of Agustin de Iturbide, were advancing daily nearer the Capitol, and driving the picked forces of Spain before them, at such a time, His Excellency the Viceroy,

The Honor of Santa Anna. 69

had every reason to look for a full attendance of los Gachupines, or his Spanish Generals.

But the chairs of Bustamente, Andrade, Quintanares, Cortazares, Negrete, Echavarri, and Novella were conspicuously vacant.

Around the official whose sun was about to set, in the political firmament, there were still gathered a faithful few, mostly line officers. There was Brigadier Linan, resplendent in a hussar uniform of blue and gold, and near him, the Brigadier Don José Davila, Captain Fernando del Valle and Lieutenant Navarrette.

" The case is desperate indeed," murmured the Viceroy, glancing at the empty chairs." " We are losing ground. Yesterday when I went upon the Plaza Grande, I was greeted with the cry, Viva el Virey—Live the peacemaker." To-day there were scowling faces and sullen silence. Dios, señores, something must be done and quickly to retrieve our arms. Shall we unite our forces against the arch traitor Iturbide, or shall we make a division and attack the forces of the lesser rebel, Santa Anna, in the south simultaneously ?"

The vote was taken in silence.

Then the Viceroy rising said :

" Brigadier Linan,—you will take a division and march immediately against Iturbide in the western provinces, Brigadier Davila, you will march at once to the southern provinces, occupy Vera Cruz, and take the rebel Santa Anna, dead or alive. If you find yourself forced to surrender the Fortress of San Juan de Uloa,

70   Iturbide, A Soldier of Mexico.

you will before capitulation, see to the instant execution of all the prisoners confined in the dungeons,— irrespective of sex. They are rebels and traitors all."

"Does your Excellency include the Captain la Garza and his wife in this order?" began the Brigadier Davila hesitatingly.

"I believe I remarked all the prisoners, irrespective of sex," replied the Viceroy dryly.

The Brigadier Linan broke in.

"Our departure leaves the Capitol almost defenseless save for the Blues and the City Guard."

"They are all-sufficient," responded His Excellency. "Besides, to-night, Captain Berdejo and the Jalapa troop will arrive, convoying a conducta of one million dollars, which will give us the means of throwing new troops into the field. And now, gentlemen of the armies of Spain, how soon can you put your forces in motion?"

"At once. The soldiers are now under arms," was the simultaneous response.

"Then go, and God speed you," said His Excellency.

The two Brigadiers saluted and left the apartment.

The Viceroy rose.

The two remaining officers saluted.

"Captain del Valle, who is stationed at the door to my library?" asked the Viceroy.

"The new recruit,—the one who comes from the southern provinces," was the reply. "He

The Honor of Santa Anna. 71

is dumb and hence the more reliable in these uncertain times when every nook and corner may conceal a spy."

"I passed the man but an hour since," said the Viceroy. "There is a familiar something about the fellow and yet I cannot place him Pity he is dumb."

"Has Your Excellency any orders?" asked Captain del Valle.

"If Captain Berdejo should arrive show him at once into the library," said His Excellency. "My writing will occupy me until morning."

The officers saluted and withdrew. The Viceroy gazed around the now silent, deserted room and put his hand before his eyes.

"Treachery and treason—daily desertions," he murmured sadly. "To-night I am His Excellency—to-morrow what?"

Opening a private door he ascended a short, onyx stairway of a few steps, leading into his library. At the door, he saw a tall hussar, with his saber at a carry, who saluted as he approached. The Viceroy gave the man a piercing glance as he passed, for there was something about the fellow that made him ill at ease.

In the library, His Excellency the Viceroy, threw himself heavily into the state chair beside the table, and after glancing at the documents with which it was littered, began a careful study of the map.

The upholstering of the library was of crim-

72 Iturbide, A Soldier of Mexico.

son satin, the furniture was of dark mahogany, and the scarlet shades of the candelabra enhanced the somber hues. A large, onyx inlaid table, was in the center of the apartment, upon which was a saber with jeweled hilt and a pair of pistols.

An hour passed—an hour of silence, broken only by the tick, tick, tick, tick, of the old clock, which had ticked for the nightly vigils of sixty-seven Spanish Viceroys.

The door opened and closed.

His Excellency looked up.

Before him stood the sentry.

With his sword at a carry, he saluted, then placed it in its sheath, and stood there in silence, his arms folded upon his breast.

"Eh—what? I did not summon you, fellow," gasped the Viceroy, with a vague alarm.

The soldier removed his helmet and the Viceroy sank back in the great chair, his brow pallid and clammy.

"Santa Anna——" he gasped.

"Santa Anna," calmly said the soldier, in a dull, hard voice.

"You are mad, man. Do you not know that with a single pull of the bell-cord, I can summon those who will lead you forth to instant execution as a spy?"

And His Excellency stretched out his hand towards the bell-cord, but there was something in Santa Anna's face, that arrested his hand.

"Why are you here?" he asked abruptly.

The Honor of Santa Anna. 73

"To obtain from you an order releasing the lady Juana la Garza, from the Fortress of San Juan de Uloa," said Santa Anna.

"And you offer in return for this?" sneered the Viceroy.

"Your life," said Santa Anna.

Then as the Viceroy again stretched his hand towards the bell-cord, Santa Anna continued:

"Excellency, we two are absolutely alone. Before your officers can come to your assistance, one or both of us will be dead."

Again His Excellency refrained from pulling the bell-cord. For he knew that Santa Anna spoke the truth.

"You offer me but small return when you offer me my life," he said earnestly. "For to a man like me my vengeance is dearer than life itself. And after all my star is on the wane. Perhaps I might hold a more honored place in history, were I to fall by the hand of Santa Anna to-night. For to-night I am still His Excellency the Viceroy of Mexico and to-night the proud banner of old Spain floats over the Capitol. But to-morrow——"

He did not complete his sentence, but buried his face in his hands.

Nor did Santa Anna speak.

Finally His Excellency resumed:

"You are a brave man, General Santa Anna, and I believe that with your support, the cause of the Bourbons will triumph in Mexico. Take the field under the Spanish banner and I will

74 Iturbide, A Soldier of Mexico.

give you the life and liberty of the woman you love."

And a crafty smile overspread the bilious face of His Excellency.

"Draw my sword for the accursed cause against which I have fought these many years —draw my sword against my brother-in arms, Iturbide? It would be dishonor, unworthy of a Mexican gentleman," cried Santa Anna.

"Dishonor—Iturbide," softly said the Viceroy with his fathomless, crafty smile. "Strange that you should link the two, my friend. They are synonymous."

"What do you mean?" asked Santa Anna.

"Will you force me to say that which will cause you regret all through your life?" asked the Viceroy.

"I do not understand Your Excellency," said Santa Anna. "Dishonor — Iturbide— synonymous? Ah God—you do not mean my little sister Dahalia? Tell me you do not mean my little sister Dahalia,— Excellency. He is to marry her. He gave me his word as a gentleman of Mexico. Madre de Dios—why does Your Excellency not speak? You are torturing me."

The Viceroy bowed his head again upon his hands, and was silent.

Santa Anna continued:

"Our dear old mother entrusted her to my care when she was but a niña—a little, toddling, innocent child. And I have watched over her and guarded her these many years. And only

The Honor of Santa Anna.   75

when I thought I was going to certain death did I entrust her to the care of the Liberator General,—a gentleman of Mexico—her affianced husband."

The Viceroy shook his head sadly.

"Do you not know that General Iturbide has a wife living in the province of Valladolid?" he asked.

With a groan Santa Anna sank into a chair, his form shaken by a great emotion.

The Viceroy could have easily summoned his officers and overpowered the man. But he thought to win him over to the cause of Spain.

After a long interval Santa Anna rose, once more himself.

"Is this the truth, Your Excellency?" he asked in a forced, unnatural voice.

"On my honor as a Spanish nobleman," replied the Viceroy, very solemnly.

"Then accursed be the day that I gave my hand in friendship to Agustin de Iturbide," said Santa Anna. "As I have labored to raise him to the supremacy of Mexico, so henceforth I shall labor to his undoing."

"And I will aid you," said the Viceroy, a great joy in his eyes. "For I will commission you a Brigadier of the Spanish line."

"Excellency—there is one thing I place above all personal feeling," replied Santa Anna gravely. "Mexico—my country. This man—Iturbide—has driven back your forces almost to the Capitol. He is on the eve of establishing the Independence of Mexico. So

76   Iturbide, A Soldier of Mexico.

be it.   The private vengeance of Santa Anna can wait.   But when this new star in the firmament shall have risen almost to the highest pinnacle of his ambition, he shall find his Santa Anna as England's Edward found his Warwick."

" Then you refuse a Brigadier's commission in our army?" said the Viceroy.   "You will fight for the cause of a man who has attainted your name with dishonor?"

" Por Dios—no," thundered Santa Anna. " Release the lady—Juana la Garza—and I pledge you my word, as a Mexican gentleman, to retire to my hacienda of Mango de Clavo, and suffer Iturbide to work out his destiny alone."

" So be it," said the Viceroy and grasped his pen.

This was a victory half gained.

When he had finished his writing, and stamped the document with the royal seal, he handed the paper to Santa Anna.

" This is the first of the month," he said. " That order will release the lady Juana la Garza from the Fortress of San Juan de Uloa on the fifteenth at high noon."

Santa Anna saluted.

" I thank Your Excellency.   I shall not forget what you have done for me this night. Henceforth Santa Anna lives but for two things—love and vengeance."

A moment and he was gone.

The Viceroy looked after him sneeringly.

The Honor of Santa Anna. 77

"Poor fool—poor fool!" he muttered. "But a moment ago you held the destiny of Mexico in your hand and you sacrificed your great opportunity for the love of a woman you will never, never see again."

Once more the door opened and closed. His Excellency looked up. Before him stood a dust-covered, haggard trooper, with downcast, livid countenance.

He saluted with his saber.

Then advanced to the Viceroy and laid it upon the table. Next tore off the gold-laced insignia of an officer of the Blues and cast them to the ground.

"Excellency——" he faltered, the tears coursing down his cheeks.

The Viceroy of Mexico sprang up and swore a great oath.

"The convoy!" he gasped, "the one million in Spanish bullion?"

"Is in the hands of Iturbide," groaned Captain Berdejo.

"Santo Dios! and the Jalapa troop—the pride of my regiment—permitted this?" shrieked the Viceroy.

"There is no longer a Jalapa troop, Excellency. They fell fighting for you," groaned the man.

"And you?" shrieked the Viceroy.

"I returned to make the only reparation a soldier can," said the Captain of the Jalapa troop. "Or else to retrieve mine honor."

"There is but one reparation you can make,"

78   Iturbide, A Soldier of Mexico.

said the Viceroy grimly.   And he took up one
of the pistols from the table.

"I am ready, Excellency," said the Captain,
folding his arms, and throwing his head back
with a new-found joy in his eyes.

The Viceroy fired.

Intentionally or otherwise he missed his aim.

The Captain of .the Jalapa troop never
moved.

The Viceroy looked at him a moment in
admiration, then tossed the pistol aside with
a bitter laugh.

"No, no, my brave Captain.   It is not such
men as you that I can spare at such a time.   I
give you your life for the present," he said.

"You give—me—my life, Excellency?"
gasped the Captain of the Jalapa troop, falling
upon his knees.   "And my pardon?"

"Not yet," replied the Viceroy, writing rapidly at the table.   "You are under sentence
of death until——"

And he finished his writing and sealed the
document with the royal arms.   Then continued—

"Until you bring me convincing proof, that
the lady Juana la Garza is dead.   Here are two
documents.   One is an order for the immediate
execution of Captain la Garza and his wife, the
lady Juana, at eleven o'clock, of the 15th day
of this month.   The other is an order for the
delivery of the body of the lady Juana la Garza
to the General Antonio Lopez de Santa Anna,
at high noon of the 15th.   You understand?"

The Honor of Santa Anna. 79

And he handed him the documents.

" I understand, Excellency," said the Captain of the Jalapa troop. " Henceforth I live but to serve you, and I shall not rest until I have seen these two enemies of my master dead."

" Bueno," said the Viceroy of Mexico sternly. " And remember, you serve me best by putting this foul, treacherous woman where she can lure no more men to ruin. Hasta la vista, pues, hasta, amigo. By riding night and day, you can reach the Fortress of San Juan de Uloa, on the evening of the 14th."

" Your orders shall be obeyed," said the Captain of the Jalapa troop. Then saluted and with an " Adios, Excellency," left the room.

When he had gone the Viceroy buried his face in his hands.

Finally:

" My cause is lost—lost irrevocably. But I think my revenge will almost be worth the loss of a one-million-dollar convoy."

80 Iturbide, A Soldier of Mexico.

CHAPTER VIII.

THE DUNGEONS OF SAN JUAN DE ULOA.

ON a rocky island commanding the city of Vera Cruz, towering skyward, stands the Castle of San Juan de Uloa, the heritage left by Hernan Cortez to the Viceroys of Mexico. Blacker than the Black Hole of Calcutta within, strongly fortified as Gibraltar without, it stood apart upon its little morro, a little hell in itself.

Loud around it roared many an angry storm. Hoarse against its crags dashed many pitiless breakers.

But all the noises of the heavens above, and of the ocean beneath could not suffice to drown the awful, pitiful, wailing shrieks of the poor wretches doomed to the misery of durance in San Juan de Uloa.

Spain has left many a bloody page on the memorials of history and when in the aftertime her name shall be called from the roll of the world's nations, there will rise in accusation against her, from her new world records, a Montezuma, an Ahatualpa, a Hidalgo, a Mina, and a host of martyrs, whose blood has served to glut the appetites of her creatures. But when the blackest page of her new world record

The Dungeons of San Juan De Uloa. 81

is scanned, methinks the name of San Juan de Uloa will stand blazoned out in letters of blood-red scarlet.

There are dungeons upon dungeons in the great military prisons of the world, but nowhere are there such dungeons as in the Fortress of San Juan de Uloa.

Situated far below the level of the sea, beneath the buttresses of the Castle, extending some sixteen feet below, their stony walls were possessed of a dank, disagreeable, fever-breeding humidity. Their floors were more or less covered with water from the sea and not infrequently great crabs and shiny jellyfish would ooze in and awaken the sleeping wretches confined there with nightmare of realism. Fetid, vaultlike odors had seasoned the gloomy life coffins, until el vomito became a frequent visitor, and the very sentries on guard shuddered and were staggered with nausea, as they opened the low doors, to toss the scant allowance to the hungry skeletons within, who tore and clawed at the bits of food like vultures quarreling over cadaverous repast. And well they might. For the rations were not many. Upon the prison records the allowance daily per capita was of bread four ounces, of rice three ounces, and of beans three.

But the venial officials of a venial nation, often curtailed this and the result was that the Fortress of San Juan de Uloa was the dwelling place of life in death. The beans and rice were always cooked in salt water, that the prisoners

82 Iturbide, A Soldier of Mexico.

might learn the lesson of economy and not yearn for second service.

Prison economy was not limited to food, but extended even to the manacles. As a means of saving space, the unfortunate wretches were chained by twos or threes or fours, men and women, arm to arm and leg to leg.

The only light came from a slit-like aperture at the top, and one hardly knew whether it was night or day.

It was night.

Deepest silence everywhere, broken by an occasional long-drawn sigh or lingering groan. Face forward on a slimy, dirty surface, a man and a woman lay, manacled to the floor. The man's face was covered by a rough beard of many days' growth, his hair, matted and unkempt, hanging in shaggy, tangled locks over his shoulders. Something cold and gristly whisked by his ear with a shrill squeak, and Captain la Garza gibbered and laughed frantically,—for long-suffering had made him mad. The lady Juana la Garza, pinioned to the floor near him, could only look and look and look with a great pity in the direction of the man whom once she had loved.

And she tried to remember the gallant young officer, in his blue and gold hussar uniform, who had led her to the altar and given her his name.

A name she had sullied with dishonor.

The man who was now a poor, unhappy fool, a vacant stare upon his face, the laugh of idiocy upon his lips, great clots of blood upon his

The Dungeons of San Juan De Uloa. 83

clothes, and upon his wrists and limbs suppurating ulcers from the cruel irons, sores in which the processes of decomposition and gangrene were already far advanced.

His sufferings must have been awful. Chained beside him was the dead, decomposing body of an old man.

Only the preceding day, the Surgeon of the Fortress had drawn up a memorial to the Governor, stating that another day under such conditions meant certain death for Captain la Garza. For the Surgeon had a spark of pity for the poor devils under his care, being still a young man and not yet hardened to such things.

But the Governor of the Fortress wrote upon the memorial,—

" Que los lleve, mientras respira."

Which is to say :

" While he breathes, he shall wear them."

And so signed the death warrant of Captain la Garza.

From overhead the great bell of the Castle tolled midnight and the slow, measured clangor sounded through the thick walls of the dungeon, like a mortuary summons.

It was the morning of the fifteenth of the month.

Gradually the wild laughter of the prisoner ceased. In his eyes shone the light of battle. In his fevered imagination he heard the rattle of musketry and the rasping clash of steel upon steel. He seemed to hear the roar of conflict

84 Iturbide, A Soldier of Mexico.

in the distance,—the curdling grito of his troopers as they swept on to the charge and carnage and conflict.

"At them, muchachos, at them," he shouted wildly. "For old Spain."

And he strove to tear himself from that merciless grip of steel,—which held him down —down—down—to the dank floor.

"For the honor of old Spain!" he cried again in clear, ringing tones.

And then died.

With every faculty strained to its utmost tension, the lady Juana la Garza lay there anxiously awaiting the first break of dawn. All sorts of uncanny terrors possessed her. She missed the gibbering of the maniac. There had been a sense of human companionship even in that awful, guttural murmuring—unintelligible though it was.

Finally, through the slitlike lattice, the weird grayish light of the dawn broke into the dungeon.

With dilated, staring eyes, the lady Juana la Garza peered into the gloom to see if her husband slept.

And when she saw the still, silent figure, suddenly came the realization that he did indeed sleep, and that his sleep was that which knows no waking.

Overcome by the horror of it all she fainted.

The Castle bell tolled ten o'clock, in mournful cadence.

The Dungeons of San Juan De Uloa. 85

It was the morning of the fifteenth.

In the Governor's room a squad of soldiers were receiving their instructions as to the conduct of the execution of two prisoners of state, which was set for eleven.

Upon the battlements, overlooking the city of Vera Cruz,—all ignorant of the preparations going on within the Governor's room,—General Antonio Lopez de Santa Anna paced restlessly to and fro, awaiting the coming of that noon, which should restore to his arms the woman he loved.

Along a dark, ill-lighted passage, the priest, Rafael Aristo, moved rapidly. For time was passing quickly, and the Governor allowed him only half an hour to confess the prisoners.

A surly turnkey preceded him and stopped before Cell No. 13, the lowermost dungeon in the tier. Inserting a great key in the rusty lock the turnkey roughly pushed the great door inwards.

The priest, Rafael Aristo, entered the dungeon.

The lady Juana la Garza looked at him with the hunted look of an animal at bay, and her whole form shook with fear.

But Rafael Aristo raised his hand in benediction, while the turnkey unlocked the manacles that held her in a vice.

" Courage, my daughter," he murmured, " I come to save you. To restore you to the arms of your lover, General Santa Anna."

" To save me ? " echoed the lady, like one in

86 Iturbide, A Soldier of Mexico.

a dream. "To restore me to General Santa Anna?"

And there was a radiant look of hope upon her wan face and a great joy in her eyes.

"Yes, my daughter," continued the priest softly. The Viceroy has ordered your execution within the next hour, and the Governor is even now making his preparations. This faithful fellow is a good Catholic and has consented to give me his aid in saving you. The passage without leads to the Santiago bastion, which is unguarded. A boat waits us there. Come, my daughter, for the time presses. Come,—to liberty and to Santa Anna."

And he supported her trembling figure upon his arm.

Together they followed the turnkey along the passage-way, and presently stood upon the Santiago bastion.

Beneath them roared, seethed, swept, advanced, retreated, the angry breakers. They dashed against the hard, irregular cliffs of San Juan de Uloa. They leaped joyously, tossing white flecks of foam in air. They crept again into the grander, vaster expanse behind. And again advanced in renewed onslaught, upon the rocky barriers.

Oh! the welcome, soothing roar of these whitecapped breakers! The inspiration of the salt sea-air!

The scintillating glint of the joyous waves was reflected by the sun-rays, athwart the gloomy fortress walls around and behind them.

The Dungeons of San Juan De Uloa. 87

When the turnkey had prepared the boat, the priest assisted the lady to a seat in the stern and the man pushed off, keeping well under the shadow of the great battlements to escape the eyes of the sentries above.

"Is it not glorious to breathe the salt air and to see grand old ocean?" asked the priest with a strange smile upon his face.

But the lady was sobbing from very excess of joy.

"My daughter, if you look to the extreme northern battlement, you will just discern the figure of a man standing erect and looking towards Vera Cruz," continued the priest, Rafael Aristo.

The lady Juana la Garza looked, but made no remark.

The priest continued:

"It is the rebel General, Antonio Lopez de Santa Anna."

And seeing the wonder in the lady's eyes, he continued:

"My daughter, I promised you a fate, far, far worse, than any death of which you could dream, if you failed us. Your imprisonment, in San Juan de Uloa, was but the beginning. The end was yet to come. Even death cannot cheat the Church of Rome of its vengeance. I, Rafael Aristo, have this day cheated death of a victim, that I might exact that retribution which the Church demands. Henceforth, there are but two persons in this world—you and myself. Over in the city yonder, two swift

88   Iturbide, A Soldier of Mexico.

horses await us.   Together we will go to the summits of the Cumbres.   You shall live with me the life of a wild beast, where no man knoweth.   At night, your bed shall be upon the open.   By day, we will climb up, up, ever up, and there shall be no rest.   So day by day, we shall travel on through the mesquit and chaparral of the Southland, fleeing in terror from the wild beasts and the reptiles everywhere abounding.   Living upon the dried bark and berries of the forest.   Up, up, up, and on, on, on, until all reason has left us and we are stark, staring mad.   Then, perhaps my heart will find that pity which it now knows not."

The priest ceased abruptly.   But in his eyes was the fierce, wild glare of the fanatic.

The woman looked long into his face, fascinated by that awful, penetrating stare.

Then, with a shriek of awful agony, would have flung herself in to the sea.

But he felled her with a swift blow.

And raising his hand, said solemnly—

" For the good of the Church of Rome."

General Don Antonio Lopez de Santa Anna saluted indifferently as Captain Berdejo joined him upon the ramparts of San Juan de Uloa.

" You come from the north, señor Capitan ? " he asked fixing the other with a penetrating glance.

" On behalf of His Excellency the Viceroy," replied Captain Berdejo brusquely.   " On much

The Dungeons of San Juan De Uloa. 89

the same business, I fancy that brings the General Santa Anna to Vera Cruz."

And Captain Berdejo winked knowingly at General Santa Anna.

" I do not understand you, señor Captain," Santa Anna replied coldly.

" Ah, so," said the other. Then tapping the papers in his belt he continued : " I fancy I have the duplicate of the document which brings the General Santa Anna to Vera Cruz. His Excellency the Viceroy makes me his executioner and makes the rebel General Santa Anna the custodian of the dead."

Santa Anna started, restrained himself and, assuming an indifference he did not feel, asked :

" Executioner ? Ah, I think I understand— I think I understand, señor Capitan. His Excellency has passed sentence upon the heretic, Captain la Garza ? "

" Not upon the man alone but upon the woman as well, General Santa Anna," replied Captain Berdejo, and produced the papers from his belt. " See, here is the sentence of death upon Captain la Garza and the lady Juana his wife, to be carried out at eleven o'clock of the morning of the fifteenth of the month. The other document is an order to the Governor of the Fortress giving into your custody the body of the lady Juana la Garza at twelve noon of the same day. Well, señor, it is just five minutes to eleven o'clock, and in five minutes this double execution will take place. My troopers are even now gone to conduct the

90   Iturbide, A Soldier of Mexico.

the prisoners to the ramparts.   I am a soldier, señor General, but am a man as well, and being a man I have known what it is to love.   I have heard of your love for the lady Juana la Garza. Perhaps I am doing what is wrong but I will take the chance.   I think the Viceroy plays you false.   My duty will I do, señor General Santa Anna, but it is my purpose to offer you a last farewell and a word in private with the woman you love."

General Santa Anna took from the hands of the other the documents as though to read them, speaking never a word.   Then stepped to the extreme end of the rampart and whistled softly.

" What—you do not accept my offer?" asked Captain Berdejo in amazement.   He thought the General Santa Anna was signaling for his boatmen.   As indeed he was.

" It will not be necessary, señor Capitan," blandly responded the rebel General.   " And yet I thank you for the service you intended."

Two score of fierce-looking Jorocho cavalry-men ascended the ramparts and ranged them-selves behind their General.   They were all armed to the teeth, their belts stuck full of pis-tols, and each brandishing a heavy saber.

At a signal from Santa Anna they took pos-session of a battery and turned the guns so that they commanded every approach to the rampart.

" What does this mean?" queried Captain Berdejo fiercely, his hand upon his sword-hilt.

The Dungeons of San Juan De Uloa. 91

" It means that there will be no execution to-day, señor Capitan," smiled Santa Anna, the gleam of the devil in his beady eyes. And he spat upon the papers of the Viceroy and threw them into the sea. " Santa Anna is not quite a fool, nor did he trust entirely to the Viceroy. I came prepared for peace or war. The Viceroy has declared war. So be it. This battery commands the powder magazines of the Fortress. Let the Governor proceed with the execution, señor, and then——"

" And then——gasped Captain Berdejo."

" Why then we'll all go to hell together," sneered Santa Anna.

He would have said more but that the bell of the castle pealed long and violently. The Governor of the Fortress appeared suddenly upon the ramparts followed by the officers of his staff.

" The prisoners— guard the prisoners ! " shouted Berdejo as he rushed towards the group of men.

" The prisoners ! " gasped the Governor, tremulous with rage. " The prisoners—cospita, señores, the prisoners have escaped. But, thank God, it is not too late. Turn the guns upon them."

And he pointed to a little speck upon the water midway between the Fortress of San Juan de Uloa and the city of Vera Cruz.

Then for the first time became aware of General Santa Anna and his Jorochos at the battery.

92   Iturbide, A Soldier of Mexico.

"In the name of the Viceroy," he cried, advancing a step.

But Santa Anna waved him back gaily with his sword.

"There is no longer a Viceroy," he shouted, with a keen note of triumph in his voice. "The Viceroy met the Emperor Iturbide at Villa Cordova last night and capitulated. And mine be the first banner of revolt raised against these double traitors. Come, gentlemen, cry with me: Viva Santa Anna. For Santa Anna is master of Vera Cruz and the Fortress of San Juan de Uloa."

Only his own devoted little band took up the cry.

Santa Anna shrugged his shoulders.

"Well, gentlemen, you do not join with me. I must ask for your swords then."

"And if we refuse?" asked the Governor half-heartedly.

Santa Anna pointed to the powder magazines. It was an excellent answer.

The Governor and his officers gave up their swords.

Santa Anna turned to Captain Berdejo whose troopers had arranged themselves around him.

"Well, amigo, you see how it is," he continued kindly. "Will you follow the rising star of General Santa Anna?"

"My life and mine honor are pledged to my Viceroy, señor General," replied the man.

"So be it," said Santa Anna. "It is not my

The Dungeons of San Juan De Uloa. 93

custom to remain long in any man's debt. You would have done me a service but a short while back. My obligation I now discharge, and give you your liberty. Go!"

He pointed to the boat in which he had come from Vera Cruz. Saluting stiffly the Captain Berdejo entered with his troopers and pushed off. Once he looked back and saw that the banner of the rebel General Santa Anna had replaced the flag of Spain.

At a meson in Vera Cruz he procured horses for himself and the troopers of his party.

" Do we join the Viceroy?" asked his lieutenant, a huge, massive man with a great black beard.

" Carramba, no," replied the Captain. "Think you I am a fool? We must follow those prisoners and carry out the will of the Viceroy before Santa Anna sets out in pursuit. As soon as he has the reinforcements he doubtless expects he will set out after that woman. I know the man."

" He will perhaps think she is safe in the hands of the priest who compassed her escape," replied the lieutenant.

" As she is, no doubt, until we overtake them," said the Captain.

" But do you seek out a Mestizo guide and we will follow on their trail even though it lead to the summit of the Cumbres. For it is my life or my lady's. So hasten, companero, the guide and then—the road again."

Saluting, the lieutenant left the meson in

94   Iturbide, A Soldier of Mexico.

quest of a Mestizo guide and as he passed the sea wall he saw upon the beach many troops of Jorocho cavalrymen and boat-load after boat-load setting out for the Fortress, of which Santa Anna was now master.

For the Church of Rome. 95

CHAPTER IX.

FOR THE GOOD OF THE CHURCH OF ROME.

ON the morning of the 27th of September, 1821, a great crush of people flocked to the southern barriers of the Capitol. There were poverty-stricken leperos, and dirty, squalid Indians, pressing ever so closely against the closed calêches, through the openings of which timidly peeped the black-robed señoras and senoritas.

Occasionally, an Aguador, with his great clay pitcher, strapped upon his back, and filled with fresh water, would elbow his way through the crowd, crying his monotonous " Agua—Agua."

Or a gaily-decked cavalier, in silver-bullioned black jacket, with gold braided zapateros, and great sombrero, wearing the colors of his señorita upon his arm, and his gaudy serape, jauntily wrapped around his gold-embossed saddle, would dig the rowels of his spurs into the foam-flecked sides of his steed, and ride down a group of affrighted children or leperos, to the great edification of the señoritas in the caleches.

Merrily rang the bells of the Cathedral.

Loud sounded the petards of the soldiery.

Occasionally a troop of Rurales would dash into the crowd with a blending of oaths, and

96 Iturbide, A Soldier of Mexico.

shouts that only added to the general confusion.

At the great Portales, flanking the Vera Cruz road, a regiment of Jalapa Infantry were drawn up, the monotony of their long wait enlivened by the martial music of the regimental band, which was at times broken in upon by the distant roll of drums, or the prolonged blowing of bugles from a distant cavalry troop.

And so it was throughout the city. In the aristocratic residence quarter, upon the overhanging terraces, could be caught glimpses of fat señoras and slender señoritas, with great wavy hair, falling over their waists, and sometimes reaching to the ground. They were belated risers, but had not foregone the customary morning toilet. And now having had their heads washed, they were drying their locks.

If one looked closer upon the terraces he might have seen some señora, of more embonpoint, or greater laziness than her sisters, enjoying her morning chocolate with perhaps a tortilla.

At the Plaza Mayor, beneath a huge triumphal arch, were the authorities of the city, in gorgeous gala uniforms—Prefects and Clergy, —then a band of white-robed little ones with floral pieces, and lastly the Ayuntamiento.

The tricolor of General Iturbide was everywhere in evidence, although occasionally might be seen the cockades of the Bourbons.

In an old-world gathering of this kind, one might have looked for more or less impatience.

For the Church of Rome. 97

But the dolce far niente Mejicano rolls his cigarette, lights it with a shrug of the shoulders and smokes.

Ayer!

Hoy!

Manana!

It is all the same. Quien sabe?

And so the good people of the Capitol elbowed each other with placid smiles, smoking the while. The cavaliers upon horseback rode over the half-naked Indians and the Indians laughed and picked themselves up and smoked again as contentedly as ever.

Presently the great guns at the southern entrance to the city told to the bystanders that the National forces, known as the Army of the Three Guarantees, were entering the Capitol.

And the corpulent señoras intent upon the advancing procession and forgetful of their dampened hair, shielded their faces with costly rebosas of finest silk, while they craned their mustached faces over the terraces. For even in bonito Mexico, some of the ladies are possessed of these luxuriant hirsute appendages.

And the lepero dropped his cigarette to clamber upon a calêche, while the fat señoras with the chocolate and tortillas, too fat to crane over the terraces could only spill their chocolate and becrumb their tortillas and fume and fret and wriggle, in vain endeavor to see the plumes at least of the passing soldiery.

The regiment of chasseurs in green and gold

7

98   Iturbide, A Soldier of Mexico.

passed by, followed successively by the troops of dragoons and hussars.   Then came a procession of black-robed priests with banners and chasubles, chanting a Te Deum.   And then the dusky, bronzed fellows of old Guerrero and the Indianos of Guadalupe Victoria.   Then the fierce-looking, " Scarlet regiment " of General Iturbide, the great black plumes upon their helmets, waving responsive to the breeze, their facings of gold braid, setting jauntily upon the scarlet, and each pair of mustaches bristling fiercely.   And they were greeted with applause more than all the others because they were the regiment of the Liberator General.

Alone were absent the Jorochos, the wiry, rough riders of the South, the daring cavalry of General Santa Anna, who, resting on their arms in the Southland, awaited only the word of their chief, to make a dash against the forces of the Liberator.

And so the troops passed on through the streets of the Capitol cheered on every side.

Some distance behind, came a high, covered diligence, drawn by ten sturdy mules with silver trappings, and driven by a fierce-looking fellow with a rough jacket, of skins, and goat zapateros, his head protected by a bullioned sombrero.   For outriders there were four buglers, who sounded the approach of their Excellencies—the Viceroy of Mexico and the Liberator General Agustin de Iturbide.

For a final battle had been fought, and the Viceroy, when his forces had been driven

For the Church of Rome.   99

almost to the sea, had met his victorious opponent at Villa Cordova, and drawn up a joint treaty, providing for a Regency of Mexico, until Spain should affirm or repudiate the contract.

Surrounding the coach, rode the swarthy-looking, gorgeously uniformed suite of His Excellency, while within the diligencia, were seated General Iturbide, the Viceroy, and Dahalia Santa Anna.

When the people beheld them there were shouts of rejoicing, and the bright cockades, tossed high in air, made a most tasty ensemble of color. The noise of rejoicing was such that their Excellencies could only doff their chapeaus and bow.

Under the great arch at the Plaza Mayor the Ayuntamiento solemnly presented General Iturbide with the keys of the Capitol. As solemnly the Liberator embraced the civic officers.

The diligencia then moved on and drew up before the Government Palace. The last of the Viceroys descended, followed by Iturbide and Dahalia.

The Clergy of the city, headed by the Archbishop, in gorgeous sacerdotal vestments, all chanting a Te Deum, preceded their Excellencies and suites into the gloomy corridors of the Palacio to the grand Salon of Ambassadors, where a magnificent banquet was in waiting.

Upon the walls of this great Salon, with its tapestry hangings, hung a choice collection of

100 Iturbide, A Soldier of Mexico.

oils from celebrated old world masters, portraits of Charles V., Ferdinand VII., Hernan Cortez, and of many of the Viceroys.

Upon the spacious tables, loaded down with every delicacy, were great pyramids of native fruits,—platanos, ananas, papayas, and zapotes, —all intermingled. And there were crystal carafes of the choicest wines, and great bowls of ices from Popocatapetl. The service of silver plate was rich and heavy and bore the royal arms of the Bourbons. Large, fragrant bouquets were at every plate.

The courses were long and tedious, but Iturbide presided with much patience, although manifestly fatigued and perturbed.

During the banquet, a party of boys and girls delighted the eyes of the guests with a measured, rhythmical Tertulia, to the slow, soft accompaniment of mandolins and guitars. And when they finally began the steps of La Habanera, a dance as dear to the Mexicans as was the minuet to the hearts of the Colonial dames, there was one great round of applause. It was during the enthusiasm incident upon La Habanera that His Excellency the Viceroy, General Iturbide, and Dahalia, made their egress from the Salon of Ambassadors to the scarlet library of the Viceroys.

A kindly-faced, stately-looking woman, in a fashionable evening costume, was telling her rosary in a secluded room of the Palace of the Archbishop of Mexico.

For the Church of Rome. 101

The time was evening.

From the National Palace, some distance away, she could hear a military band discoursing patriotic airs. And her heart was glad. For Madame de Iturbide had come by special diligence, post-haste, from her villa at Valladolid to see her husband's triumphant entry into the Capitol.

The stately, saintlike woman had felt no twinge of suspicion or jealousy at her husband's seeming neglect, since she knew that he was a soldier of Mexico.

A door leading into the apartment opened and one of the ladies in waiting entered noiselessly and stood respectfully until her mistress should speak.

"Approach, Nita," said Madame de Iturbide kindly.

"Señora, His Eminence the Archbishop of Mexico, Cardinal del Fonte, attended by his seven suffragans, craves an audience."

"I will see him, Nita," said Madame de Iturbide, and the girl withdrew.

A moment later the Archbishop entered, looking grandly severe in his red simar and laces.

His Eminence raised his hand in benediction over Madame de Iturbide.

"I have brought my suite as an escort for you, Madame."

"As an escort? I fail to understand, your Eminence," murmured Madame de Iturbide.

"To conduct you to the Imperial Palace,"

102 Iturbide, A Soldier of Mexico.

replied the Archbishop. "Since your husband comes not to you, it is obvious that you must go to him and assume your proper place at his side."

"He is busied with affairs of state," said Madame de Iturbide. "And will come to me at his own good time."

"Say rather with affairs of love, Madame," replied his Eminence gently. "Few secrets can be hidden from the Church, and I say that if it is not already too late, it is your duty to save your husband from dishonor. God knows, I would have spared you this. But the path of duty forces me to speak, though rather plainly. Your husband, though admittedly a great man in those affairs pertaining to the sword and politics, is weak where it comes to his affections. For some months he has been thrown into constant association with the Señorita Dahalia Santa Anna."

"Yes," gasped Madame de Iturbide, paling and pressing her hand to her side.

"And under the promise of a marriage he can never fulfil he is leading the girl on to her ruin. You alone can save her to-night by taking your proper place at your husband's side. So come, Madame, and tear the veil from this young girl's eyes. Then, if I know the Santa Annas, her love will turn to hate, and she will leave the man who has attainted her young name with dishonor. She will leave him and go to her brother in the Southland."

"And when she has told him all, turn the

For the Church of Rome. 103

forces of Santa Anna, like unleashed bull-dogs, upon my husband," added Madame de Iturbide. —" And with Santa Anna and Iturbide arrayed against each other, the forces of the Viceroy will easily recover their lost ground, and the liberty of Mexico, crushed to earth, will be but a short-lived dream. Ah, no, no, it shall not be the wife of the Liberator General that sets upon him the cavalry of Santa Anna in the South, in the hour of his triumph. It is far, far better that I return to the solitude of my villa, and suffer my husband to exhaust this fleeting passion. Time and time alone will bring Agustin back to me, and until then my love must rest in abeyance for the good of Mexico."

"And I say that your love must assert itself this night for the good of the Church of Rome," said the Archbishop, sternly, his eyes shining with the wild light of fanaticism. For the Archbishop knew that, when Santa Anna should once raise the banner of rebellion, the cause of Iturbide was irrevocably lost, and the Viceroy,—puppet of the Church,—would come into his own again.

"For the good of the Church of Rome?" gasped Madame de Iturbide.

"Yes, señora," said His Eminence, sternly, "and if you separate not this man and this woman, the one from the other, to-night,—por Dios, I'll hurl against your husband's cause the bans of the Church of Rome, and I need not tell you that the cause of the excommunicated is a lost cause."

104 Iturbide, A Soldier of Mexico.

" Ah—Dios—excommunication," shrieked Madame de Iturbide. " No, no, not that, not that,—I will bow to the will of your Eminence,—even though it means my husband's everlasting hate."

"Come, then, Madame," said the Archbishop. And there was the light of triumph in his eyes as he gently took her hand in his and led her to the door. " Come to the Palace and order this girl from your husband's presence. It is now half-past eight. We should reach the Imperial Palace at nine. And be brave, my daughter, be brave. Remember that what you are about to do is for the good of the Church of Rome."

CHAPTER X.

THE CONVERSION OF A WOMAN-HATER.

Upon the highest portion of the Mexican Cordilleras, far above the cloud line, the vegetation is sparse and scattered, and the only relief from the monotony and bleakness all abounding, are occasional patches of pitiful, half-dried magueys, interspersed with mesquit or half-nourished nopal. The mountain peaks of the Cumbres consist of a series of barrancas, with scarce a footpath for the wolf or mountain lion, let alone for man.

Yet on a certain moonlight night in the early fall, two human figures crouched before a scant fire on the highest peak of the Cumbres. Two figures—a man and a woman—both gaunt and haggard, from long exposure to the elements. Their garments were torn and tattered to threads, from contact with the underbrush of the Cumbres. Their feet were bare, cut and bleeding. The moon smiled serenely down upon the mountain tops, and by its clear light could be seen far below, endless slopes and the tropic vegetation of the lowlands. But above was nothing but the cloudless sky, star-flecked and clear, and seeming to cry out upon the pitiful works of man.

The woman gnawed at a piece of dried bark

106 Iturbide, A Soldier of Mexico.

with the ravenous interest of a wild beast. The man crouched close over the feeble fire.

"I am cold," he muttered with chattering teeth. "Cold—cold—cold."

But the woman gnawed at the bark and paid no attention.

"I am cold," repeated the man, and this time he struck her across the face with his whip.

Mechanically the woman removed the faded scarlet vest she wore and handed him. He wrapped it around his shoulders and continued to crouch over the fire, cursing and muttering to himself.

And the woman gnawed at the bark.

A great shaking came upon the man and his teeth came together like castanets.

"I am cold," he repeated again. And again he struck her. She removed her soft, embroidered chemise, and this also she wrapped around him. Save for a tattered silk petticoat, and an undergarment of merino, the body of the woman was exposed entirely to the crisp, biting winds of the uplands. And yet she did not seem to mind the bleak, piercing blasts, but gnawed at the strip of bark incessantly. Upon the beautiful back with its rounded curves accentuated in the play of the moonbeams, great welts, livid and marked, stood out. But upon the woman's face, which had once been strikingly beautiful, suffering had placed a restfulness that gave a glimpse into the hereafter and made her seem as one of those of whom the poet said:

The Conversion of a Woman-Hater. 107

" One spirit in them ruled, and every eye
Glared lightning and shot forth pernicious fire
Among the accursed, that withered all their strength,
And of their wonted vigor left them drained,
Exhausted, spiritless, afflicted, fallen."

Out on the night air resounded a pitiful, prolonged wail, like the cry of a lost soul, or the plaintive tremor of a little child. And the woman shivered, though not from the cold, and with trembling hands added fuel to the flames. For the cry was that of the coyote, midnight marauder, whose baleful eyes peered ravenously from the mesquit of the barranca upon the two intruders upon the silent mountain wilderness,—the coyote whose sharp, ravenous teeth were only balked of their feast of human flesh, by the flickering light of the camp-fire.

Oblivious to the woman and the coyote, the man sank down beside the fire and fell into a troubled slumber. And even in his sleep he tossed and shook and moaned and cried out upon the cold. For the fever of the hot lands, bred of the miasma of the Cumbres, was upon him and his mind was wandering.

All night the woman sat by the feeble fire, dry-eyed and careless, mechanically adding fuel, when it died down, and gnawing at her strip of bark. And all unconscious of her nakedness.

Once when the wind was cutting, with a more than usual fierceness, she loosed the gray-streaked, heavy, luxuriant tresses, and

108 Iturbide, A Soldier of Mexico.

they fell, in great profusion, down and around her shoulders giving her the appearance of a wild, affrighted nymph of the forest. So through the night.

Gradually, over the surface of the neighboring barrancas, appeared the first luminous streaks of the morning and the woman was glad, for the night had been a night of horror. High in the east appeared the rose-red sun, and the early morning breezes, ascending from below, brought with them the fragrant aroma of the wild lupins and marigolds, from the primeval stretch of woodland below. Once a tiny guardia-bosque, having soared higher than his wont, flitted timidly near the woman, who glanced at his rich blue plumage, with lack-luster eyes.

Only the foolish babbling of the sleeping man seemed to arouse her, as he moaned and tossed in his fever like a great helpless infant.

She mechanically seized his great shovel hat, which had fallen from his head, and clambering, with a recently-acquired agility, from rock to rock, she swept into it with her little hand stagnant water lurking in their crevices. Then gathering the little berries from the dwarfed mesquit bushes, all-abounding, she crushed them into a pulp, with her slender, delicate fingers, and tossed them into the hat with the water.

Then she aroused her companion, who glared at her with listless, apathetic eyes and placed the hat to his lips that he might drink,

The Conversion of a Woman Hater. 109

while with her other hand she stroked his matted locks, and murmured sweet empty nothings in his ears.

For she was a woman. And more, she had suffered in the dungeons of San Juan de Uloa.

When he had taken a long, deep draught of the concoction, he handed her the hat and sank down to sleep again. And the woman gnawed her bark, and drank some of the nauseous stuff and then sat there rubbing the man's fevered head. So the day passed. And then another night of horror. And then another day.

Still the man rolled and tossed, but manifested less delirium. Her hand upon his forehead seemed to exercise a cooling, soothing influence.

Once, as she bended over him, she saw in his belt a stiletto, such as priests were wont to carry in the troublous times of war. A baneful light came into her eyes, for her memory was awakened. And she grasped it by the hilt, and drew it from its sheath.

With an effort she poised it over his head.

The fever-stricken man was talking in his sleep and the woman paused to listen. There was time enough for vengeance.

" Viva Mejico—The Church of Rome—*hasta la eternidad*—the Church of Rome."

The stiletto dropped from the woman's hand.

" No—-no—I cannot murder a delirious man,

110 Iturbide, A Soldier of Mexico.

even though he has been my worst enemy," she muttered, and resumed her lonely vigil at his side.

Upon the morning of the sixth day the light of reason came to Rafael Aristo. He looked upon the lady Juana la Garza and there was sadness in his eyes.

"Oh ! I have dreamed such horrible accursed dreams," he moaned feebly. "Blood—blood—blood, and the smoke of battle, the cries of dying men, patriot and royalist locked in fierce embrace, all have I seen in mine awful, terrifying visions. And then I have seen the sabers of the patriot chiefs turned upon each other, and seen their armies driven to inevitable destruction, by internecine strife and petty jealousies. Sometimes a momentary flash of reason revealed to me an angel, bending over me and stroking my aching head. And when I looked into the face of my beneficent genius I saw the lady Juana la Garza, and, just behind her, the face of my dear old mother, stern and angry,—who shook her gray head in menace, and drew under her protecting arm the form of my good angel. Oh, my lady, take up the stiletto, and kill me, for I have well deserved it after the long weeks of hell I have caused you."

"I forgive you all, Rafael Aristo," said his companion sadly, "for you too have suffered." And the eyes of the priest were wet with moisture, and very humbly he kissed her hand.

The Conversion of a Woman-Hater. 111

Quick passed the day and after it another. And with the coming of yet another day the priest was stronger and sought in many ways how he might make more comfortable his companion.

For the first time since his convalescence, he noticed that her bosom and beautiful shoulders were devoid of covering. Just between her two milk-white breasts, he saw a green bag suspended from her neck by a slender gold chain, and he remembered that she was a daughter of the Church.

As he bended almost touching her, the volatile, sensuous woman aroma, emanating from her palpitating bosom, entered into his nostrils and filled him with a feeling, strange, new and indescribable. A dainty wisp from her beautiful tresses, brushed his forehead and sent a savory thrill throughout his trembling form.

" Kill me—kill me ! " he cried, tearing himself by an almost superhuman effort of the will, from the first animal instinct engendered by the love of woman, and regarding her with hungry, wistful, devouring eyes. Then for the first time noticing the great livid welts upon her shoulders,—welts that he himself had caused in his mad delirium he drew her forcibly to him, and although she struggled frantically in his fierce embrace, he rained down upon her swanlike neck, a passionate, ardent shower of hot, fevered, burning, soulful kisses.

"Love me—love me ! " he cried, in an agony of emotion,—pressing her the closer to

112 Iturbide, A Soldier of Mexico.

him, while the red blush, of shame circled her cheeks in a hectic flush making her seem like that Juana la Garza who had held sway at Apodaca's court, as the most beautiful woman in Mexico.

"Release me—release me!" she panted, breathing heavily. "Else by the Mother of God, your stiletto shall bury my shame— Remember—you are a priest of the Church of Rome."

"Love me—love me!" panted Rafael Aristo tearfully. "You have awakened within me my manhood—your contact tells me that there is something more to live for than the Church— the love of woman. Love me—love me—and I swear by the Virgin that I will make up to you the loss of Santa Anna. I am a Jesuit and can sway these puppets at will. You shall have wealth, position, and all that the Church of Rome can give. Outwardly I will be what the world demands—the sleek and unctuous Churchman, but for your sake that I can give to my mistress all that she could ask and more, for your sake, I will forswear my vow of celibacy and condemn my soul to eternal hell hereafter, my love, my life."

And once again he showered his burning, passionate kisses upon her palpitating bosom. But she repulsed him and would have snatched the stiletto but that the love-frenzied, amorous priest bore her to the ground and holding her in tight embrace pressed his hot, fevered lips against hers.

The Conversion of a Woman-Hater. 113

"Love me—love me!" he gasped hoarsely and drew her closer to him. But the woman struggled, and struggling there upon the mountain-top her skirt and kirtle became detached and fell to the ground. For the first time in all his life Rafael Aristo beheld all the gloried outlines of one of Nature's masterpieces—a woman in the nude. The ivory white, palpitating breasts, the rounded hips, superb in every contour, the thin, tapering waist of a Venus de' Medici, the glorious, statuesque limbs, all awakened in the man a thousand devils. The rose-red umbilic circlet, a beautiful little dot in the linea alba half hidden by the rising and falling of the muscular creases, acted upon Rafael Aristo as a fetich, and he drank in the wondrous beauty of the woman with eyes staring, fixed. Once in the long ago, in Rome, he remembered having seen among the paintings of the old masters, just such another little navel which had held him spellbound, until he brought himself to the realization that his fetich was only a creation upon canvas. Now the old sensation was reawakened within him. There is in every woman an inherent attribute of mind or body which never fails to act as an irresistible charm upon men. The resonant chord in the mind of Rafael Aristo was touched by the perfect, dimpling umbilic of the woman before him. He would have conquered her but for the weakness in which his fever had left him. As it was, exhausted, he fell back weak and trembling, his whole form quivering with

114 Iturbide, A Soldier of Mexico.

newly enkindled emotion. Amorous though weak, he could only look and look and look.

The woman grasped the stiletto, yet mindful of her nakedness quickly veiled all the wondrous loveliness of Nature with her kirtle. And her cheeks were flaming—hot. For the lady Juana La Garza was not yet wholly wanton.

"Ah God—relieve me of this love fever, else I perish," gasped the priest with quivering lips.

"It is your punishment," said the woman sternly. "'Tis but a few years, since I was a pure, innocent child-woman, happy in my husband's love and you—pimp and pander of the Viceroy that you were—you forced me to sacrifice my honor for the good of the Church of Rome. But know that the very hell on earth you have caused me to suffer, in the last few months, has cleansed my soul and made me something more than a thoughtless toy to gratify man's lust in the pleasure of the moment. It remained for you, Rafael Aristo, to make me ashamed that I am a daughter of the Church. But I will end it all now."

And she pressed the point of the stiletto upon her palpitating bosom.

"Stop—stop!" cried the priest with alarm in his eyes.

"Then swear by your hope of eternal salvation to speak no word of love to me again," said the lady Juana La Garza earnestly.

"I swear it by the Virgin," replied Rafael

The Conversion of a Woman-Hater. 115

Aristo, crossing himself and looking at her with fearful, anxious eyes.

She threw the stiletto upon the ground.

"Henceforth I am your sworn slave—you have but to command and I obey," continued the priest.

"I shall trust you," said the lady Juana La Garza. "Do you know where the Convent of Santa Teresa lies from here?"

"Some leagues below, in the foothills," replied the priest. "I think I can find the way. Yet assuredly you will not become a veiled nun and immure your beauty in a living tomb?"

"Yes," responded the lady. "My beauty has been to me a fatal curse and I am awearied of the world and its intrigues. I sigh only for some secluded spot where the veil will hide my features from the lustful gaze of men."

"But this is wrong," said the priest, "and I will not permit it."

"Remember your oath," said the lady.

"I do and already I repent it," said the priest, mournfully.

The lady la Garza, again picked up the stiletto. But Rafael Aristo, with difficulty rising to his feet, said :

"Since you wish it we will go to the Convent of Santa Teresa."

"You are too weak at present," said the lady.

"We must go nevertheless," he replied.

"And why?" asked the lady.

For answer he pointed to the slopes below.

116 Iturbide, A Soldier of Mexico.

His keen Indian eyes had detected what the lady would not have noticed.

She shaded her eyes with her hand.

Far down the Cumbres the rays of the early morning sun fell upon the black plumed helmets of a few blue-jacketed troopers, who were with difficulty making the ascent behind a Mestizo guide.

" The troopers of the Viceroy are coming to carry out the sentence of death, from which I saved you at Vera Cruz. But we will baffle them. Once in the Convent of Santa Teresa, you are saved. For they dare not profane the house of God."

" They will not hesitate to follow me even into the sanctuary if the Viceroy wills it," replied the lady wearily ; " for the Viceroy has no heart nor does he fear God, man or devil. His vengeance will never rest until I have been sacrificed. But we will nevertheless attempt to evade these men who have been so long pursuing us. For I do not think I am quite ready to die just yet."

" Come then," said the priest, " for I am now become a man, and for the love of woman, which I have never known until now, I would peril my very soul. You shall be saved, though all the armies of the Viceroy and all the devils in hell were pursuing, for the Church of Rome protects you."

And taking her little hand in his he led her on through the chaparral of the barranca, and away from the helmeted dragoons on the slopes below.

Compliments of General Santa Anna. 117

CHAPTER XI.

THE COMPLIMENTS OF GENERAL SANTA ANNA.

THE old clock in the Imperial Palace was giving its measured tick, tick, tick, tick, as it had ticked for the sixty-seven Spanish Viceroys, as it had ticked for Don Juan Apodaca, on his last night of power—so now it was ticking for the last of the Excellencies and for General Agustin de Iturbide, the man of the future, and for Dahalia Santa Anna. There were the same somber scarlet tapestries, the same somber mahogany furniture with its scarlet upholsterings, the same onyx inlaid table, with its state papers, the great secret panel with hidden spring, known only to the last of the Viceroys.

The hands of the old clock pointed to a quarter to eight.

Dahalia was curled upon a divan, in a distant corner of the library, a kind of oratory, which shut her off from the main apartment. She was reading Don Quixote, and its pages did not evidently interest her greatly, for from listening to the faint hum of the two Generals in conversation, she fell gradually into a doze. She was fatigued, for the last few days had been most taxing upon all the party.

118 Iturbide, A Soldier of Mexico.

El Generalissimo Agustin de Iturbide was perusing a war map. His Excellency the Viceroy was seated by a small table, upon which was a decanter with glasses, and a silver brazero, of live coals, from which he lighted many cigars, for His Excellency was a great smoker.

"I must conciliate Santa Anna," said Iturbide thoughtfully.

"Of necessity, for he can be useful," replied His Excellency. "But how will you bring it about?"

"By creating him a General of the Southern provinces and conferring upon him my cross of the Order of Guadalupe," replied Iturbide.

"Cospita, señor Generalissimo," said the Viceroy, blowing a great cloud of smoke from his cigar. "Think you a commission and a decoration will repay a man like Santa Anna for the loss of his sister's honor?"

Iturbide started as though to have made some sharp retort, then remembering that the Viceroy was his guest he controlled himself and finally said:

"Your Excellency joins with the world in condemning what is little more than a Platonic association."

"Because I believe with the world that such a relationship, between a man and a woman is impossible," said the Viceroy frankly.

"And yet when I assure you on my honor as a gentleman of Mexico that never in thought or act have I failed in the trust bestowed upon

Compliments of General Santa Anna. 119

me by General Santa Anna, when I assure you that Dahalia, his sister, is as pure as when I first met her——"

" I believe you, on such assurance," said the Viceroy, " but the world—and Santa Anna himself—ah, my friend, you will find it less easy to convince them."

There was a knock at the door.

" Pase!" said Iturbide, rising. A chasseur of the guard entered.

" A courier from General Santa Anna at Vera Cruz, seeks an immediate audience," said the chasseur,

" Bid him enter," said Iturbide.

The chasseur saluted and withdrew.

" Strange that we should be talking of General Santa Anna, at the moment his courier is entering the gates of the Palacio," said Iturbide.

" I look for stranger things than that on this night," replied the Viceroy musingly.

" Your Excellency speaks in riddles," replied Iturbide.

" To you, perhaps, yes," responded the Viceroy. " And you must pardon the weakness of a superstitious man. It is my birthnight and its every anniversary has been to me fruitful of evil and misfortune. My mother died on the night of my coming into the world,—my father was assassinated on its anniversary, two years later. My only son was drowned at sea, five years ago to-night. And I have always felt a superstitious fear of my birthnight since,

120 Iturbide, A Soldier of Mexico.

being the last of my family and the last of the King's Viceroys."

"Mere coincidences," said Iturbide. "And this one birthnight in particular you were never more free from danger. My chasseurs guard every entry to the Imperial Palace. You are my honored guest. So banish fear and——"

A renewed knocking. The same chasseur entered and after saluting announced:

"The courier from General Santa Anna to the Generalissimo Iturbide."

A priest entered. The chasseur saluted.

"Let no one disturb me to-night under any circumstances," said Iturbide.

The chasseur withdrew.

"He signs his own death-warrant," mused the priest. And there was a sinister gleam in his little beady eyes. His costume consisted of a long black robe, the silver cross and rosary of his order at his belt, while in his hand he held a three cornered black hat. Even so, he seemed more soldier than priest.

The old clock of the Viceroys struck eight.

"From Vera Cruz, your reverence?" asked Iturbide, resuming his seat and lighting a cigar from the brazero.

"From the camp of General Antonio Lopez de Santa Anna," replied the priest.

"And General Santa Anna rests his soldiery at Vera Cruz?" continued Iturbide.

"For the present the forces of Santa Anna encamp at Vera Cruz, señor Generalissimo, until he knows your Excellency's will," replied

Compliments of General Santa Anna. 121

the priest. "But he sends a bottle of priceless old wine, that you may know his heart is in your cause. And he begs you to drink, to-night, with the compliments of General Santa Anna."

And the priest produced from under his robe, a quaint looking carafe, with every appearance of great age and a cobweb envelope. This he set upon the table by the Viceroy, whose lips smacked in anticipation.

"Cospita—señor Generalissimo," said the Viceroy. "In faith, I am a Royalist, but for the sake of this good old wine, I will right gladly drink a toast to the rebel General Santa Anna."

And he opened the carafe and filled two glasses. He was about to fill a third, but the priest shook his head.

"I care not for wine, Your Excellency," he said gravely.

The Viceroy set down the carafe. The priest walked over to the war map, and began to study it, with his back towards them. He wished to hide from his victims the wild gleam of ferocious joy in his eyes.

The two Generals, each took a glass and held it to the light to see the mellow sparkle in the limpid, liquid depths. It seemed to cast off a hundred scintillations in the scarlet reflection from the candelabra. One might have fancied that the green monster of the wormwood lay sleeping in the dazzling elixir. And Dahalia slept in the little oratory, all unconscious that the shadow of the Yerba Loco, hung

122   Iturbide, A Soldier of Mexico.

heavy like a pall over the scarlet library of the Viceroys.

There was the sound of steel clashing upon steel in the patio.

"A street brawl," muttered Iturbide.

The chasseur of the guard burst in unceremoniously.

"A troop of the Reds, are fighting the chasseurs of the Palace Guard, señor Generalissimo," he cried excitedly. "And our Colonel begs that you quell the riot by showing your presence in the patio."

"Riot—carramba—it is more than a riot from the noise," cried Iturbide drawing his saber.

The Viceroy rose with his hand upon his sword, but Iturbide motioned him to his seat. The clash of sabers resounded through the corridors of the Palace and the voices of men in the agony of mortal combat.

"No—no—your Excellency," said Iturbide. "You are my guest. Stay and drink the health of Santa Anna and I will return when I have stopped these maudlin roysterers."

With this the Generalissimo rushed from the library sword in hand followed by the chasseur of the guard.

The last of the Viceroys stood looking after him uncertainly, his hand upon his sword-hilt.

"The regency of Iturbide begins with bloodshed," he murmured.

"And it will end with bloodshed," said the priest prophetically.

Compliments of General Santa Anna. 123

"Eh? What did you say?" asked the Viceroy.

"I said it would be maintained by the sword," replied the man.

"Your reverence is right," said the Viceroy. "But sufficient unto the day is the evil thereof. And now for the wine. In truth I will drink a toast, but instead of drinking to the rebel General Santa Anna I will drain a glass to the patriot General Iturbide."

And very gracefully the Viceroy emptied his glass.

"And may his reign be as the effects of the wine you have drained," said the priest with a sneer upon his face.

"And how is that?" asked the Viceroy.

"Short and quick," sneered the priest.

"You mean——?" shouted the Viceroy.

"I mean that you have drank of the deadly Yerba Loco," hissed the priest, his face wild with passion and hatred. "That Santa Anna has chosen me as the humble instrument for the working of his will."

"Mother of God!" groaned the Viceroy, pressing his hand to his heart, "It is killing me now. My body is being consumed by the fires of hell—I am going blind—my head is bursting. For God's mercy tell me the antidote, if there is a spark of human feeling in your breast."

And the Viceroy clutched the table in his mad agony for support.

"Upon one condition," hissed the priest.

"And it is?"

124 Iturbide, A Soldier of Mexico.

"Open the secret panel of the Viceroys," replied the priest.

"Lead me to it then," gasped the Viceroy, "I am almost blinded, I am going mad, I am going mad."

Quickly the priest seized the Viceroy's arm and supporting him led him as he directed to the panel. With trembling fingers the Viceroy felt along the wall and finally touched the secret spring.

With a loud click the panel flew open.

The priest released the Viceroy's arm.

"The antidote—the antidote!" gasped His Excellency.

"The antidote? Why, carramba, Excellency, the antidote is death," sneered the priest, and sprang into the passage-way.

Then the Viceroy closed the door upon him and reeled back, laughing wildly.

"Mother of God—this is my last birthnight to be sure, but it is the last message you will bear for General Santa Anna, señor priest. You know not of the grating at the other end of the passage. Go—find it—rot there until your damned, treacherous body is but a mass of corruption. Rave! Rave! Rave! Storm and tear your hair in the horrors of suffocation. Beat upon unanswering walls. The secret of the panel dies with the last of the Viceroys. I had intended it for the rebel Iturbide tonight, but his fate I give to you in exchange for the Yerba Loco."

And with a terrible laugh the last of the

"Open the secret panel of the Viceroys," replied the priest.
Page 124.

Compliments of General Santa Anna. 125

Viceroys threw himself upon the floor and began to tear and scratch at the heavy carpet in his agony.

The heavy fall awakened Dahalia from her sound sleep! She rushed from the oratory in affright. She glanced around the scarlet library of the Viceroys. There was no one to be seen. Only the sound of voices in the corridor. Only a nameless, incessant scratching, that made her flesh creep weirdly. The girl glanced at the little table with its carafe. She saw the carafe. She saw the glass of sparkling wine that the Viceroy had poured for Iturbide. She drained it and set the glass upon the table with trembling hand.

" I am all unnerved," she muttered.

The faint scratching continued, and something like a groan echoed through the apartment. It was this that guided the trembling Dahalia, to the prostrate body of the Viceroy, twitching in the throes of an awful agony. With wild, dilated eyes, she started back and shrieked :

" Help, Agustin—help—there has been murder done here—help!"

And then she heard the answering cry of Iturbide, the tramping of many feet in the corridor, and she reeled faintly against the wall, with glazing eyes, for the deadly Yerba Loco, was working God's will upon the sister of General Antonio Lopez de Santa Anna.

When Iturbide re-entered the scarlet library of the Viceroys, attended by the officers of his

126 Iturbide, A Soldier of Mexico.

suite, who had rallied to him, from every corridor, a strange and fearful sight met his eyes, and for a moment he stood as though bound by the glamour of a spell. In one corner lay a huddled, immobile mass, scarce bearing the semblance of humankind,—the body of a man in a rich court costume of black velvet, his hands clutching convulsively at the thick carpet, his locks tangled in confusion, his wild dilated eyes almost popping from their orbits, looking like great red balls of fire, his lips cyanotic, with a whitish-blue, foam-flecked, and his face already black as from the talon of a strangler.

And the great clock was ticking its measured strokes for the final birthnight of His Excellency.

Near an overturned table Dahalia had fallen to the floor. Her great beautiful hair fell in luxuriant masses over her shoulders.

Through the folds of her evening dress her beautiful bosom was revealed, of an alabaster whiteness, rising and falling, in quick, palpitating undulations. There was an agonized flexion of her slender fingers, accentuated by a fast-gathering tint of blue discoloration. Her face was wan and pinched and yellowish in hue and her cyanosed lips twitched convulsively. Only her eyes were brighter and more dilated as if unwilling to yield to impending dissolution, and in them was a look of unutterable horror, as if she were the victim of an awful hallucination.

Compliments of General Santa Anna. 127

"Dahalia—my darling—speak to me—for God's sake speak to me," moaned Iturbide, oblivious of everything but the delirious girl whose brow was already damp with the dew of death.

His voice seemed to rouse her, for she raised her head, with those wildly staring death's eyes, and repulsing his caresses she began to slowly crawl, upon her hands and knees, to the panel where lay the stiffened body of the Viceroy in his court costume of black.

Iturbide watched her with his hand upon his burning brow.

Slowly the delirious girl dragged herself across the room, slowly and painfully, step by step, her body shaken by repeated spasmodic convulsions, her face already set,—only those wondrous, flashing eyes bespeaking life.

With those awful, flexed, bluish fingers, she grasped the shoulders of the Viceroy, and bending over until her face almost touched the black, discolored features of His Excellency, she stared long and earnestly as one drawn by an awful fascination, into his great, blood-circled, protruding eyes, with their sunken orbits, and black rings, the only coloring in the mass of dissolution.

Long she stared and then raising her head, with a swift convulsive movement, she said in a hard, metallic voice, that seemed to emanate from the depths of a vault:

"I have seen upon the retina of His Excellency, the accursed features of his murderer,

128 Iturbide, A Soldier of Mexico.

bespeaking hate and assassination, and the insensate love of the Yerba Loco. I have seen the same accursed features livid and staring from an awful suffocation, in yon secret passage of the Viceroys. I have seen him clutching at his throat, rending his hair in dire anguish and dashing his fists frantically against the great walls of the barred passage-way,—for the good God has placed in the eyes of the victim the picture of His awful vengeance, and gives me the knowledge, that the murderous priest, is even now gasping in the last throes of a grim, horrible death. Near him lies the decomposed, putrid body of another victim of God's will and the priest is tearing at the dead flesh in his agony of soul. He shrieks in his despair. He blasphemes and his utterance chokes from an awful fear, for he feels the weight of God's hand, exacting an awful retribution. The chill of death has seized upon his limbs. It is creeping up—up—up—slower —quicker—quicker, almost to his heart. He shrieks. The death-rattle sounds and sticks in his throat. He clutches at the silent dead man at his side and, with a long, low gasp of horror, —dies. That is the picture God gives me, Agustin. And now I see the sea, with its great, rolling breakers and the glint of the sand upon the shore. A ship is tossing at anchor in the harbor. There are soldiers upon the beach, and Agustin, erect and proud, my Agustin standing alone. His eyes are blinded by the tricolor. His hands are bound. They raise

Compliments of General Santa Anna. 129

their muskets. Madre de Dios—it is an execution—no, no, no, they shall not shoot. Stop, stop, stop, Agustin, my life, my love, my Emperor." *

With a wild shriek she fell prone upon the floor.

Iturbide rushed to her side and raised her head, looking into her glazed expressionless eyes.

Then letting it fall and bowing his head upon his hands he sobbed:

" Dead—Dahalia dead—ah, little niña, speak just one word of love—give me one sign of recognition—one little reminder, that may soften the memory of this awful night. Dead—ah

---

* " A mediados de Julio llego Iturbide a Soto la Marina y Beneski recibio orden de desembarcar el primero e investigar el estad de la opinion y la disposicion de los espiritus.—El dia 19 de Julio (1824) D. Felipe de la Garza se presento al Sr. Iturbide y le dijo friamente que estaba preso, y que el congreso habia resuelto que fuese pasado por los armas en virtud de la ley que le declaraba proscripto. Inutiles fueron todas las reflecsiones que hizo el desgraciado caudillo : inutiles sus protestas, sus razonamientos, el recuerdo de sus servicios, de aquellos servicios cuyo fruto era la independencia del pais, y la ecsistencia de aquellas mismas autoridades que le condenaban. Cinco diputados habian pronunciado la sentencia de su muerte, ejerciendo el poder judicial de la manera mas inaudita y atroz. EL HEROE DE IGUALA fue fusilado en la plaza publica de Padilla, a presencia de un pueblo lleno de estupor. Antes de morir echsorto a los que le escuchaban a obedecer las leyes y procurar la paz, y suplico que se respetase a su esposa, cuya situacion reclamaba la compasion de todo hombre que no hubiese perdido toda la sensibilidad de que la naturaleza doto a la especie humana."——

" Ensayo Historico de las Revoluciones de Mexico."
Por D. Lorenzo de Zavala. (Mexico, 1845.)

9

130 Iturbide, A Soldier of Mexico.

Dios—grant her one little brief moment of consciousness that her eyes may look into mine with the old look of love, with the old look of stainless purity and innocence. Dahalia dead —ah—no, no, no—God will not be so cruel as to take her from me—speak, my little nina, speak, chiquita—only come back to me for one little moment of love—for one little brief moment of life—and I will give up all my armies my honors, my country, my life. Dahalia dead—my God! thou art cruel to me this night, unless thou takest me too. Dead—dead—the Viceroy dead—Dahalia dead—the accursed poisoning priest dead—and only Iturbide lives —only Iturbide lives—and for what? My love has died to-night, and my ambitions have been crushed. For what then? With Dahalia it might have been Augustin the Good, the Just, the Great. Without Dahalia, it will be Agustin the Reckless, the Cruel, the Despairing."

And the Emperor of Mexico broke down and sobbed like a child, and his body was shaken by the violence of his emotions. His grief was that mighty, all-consuming grief which comes but once in a lifetime to strong self-contained men.

From far down the corridor of the Palacio there came a solemn chanting, in mournful cadences, the chanting of the suffragans, those grim, gloomy, black-robed attendants of His Eminence, the Archbishop of Mexico.

Iturbide knelt beside the body of Dahalia, weeping, and never raised his head as His Em-

Compliments of General Santa Anna. 131

inence appeared at the doorway of the salon, in his red simar and laces, leading Madame de Iturbide by the hand and followed by the seven, grim, shaven men in black, still chanting the mournful music of the Church of Rome.

His Eminence made the sign of the cross. Madame de Iturbide, taking all the terrible scene at a glance, crossed over to her husband, raised him gently, and led him to a chair as she would have led a little child. Then unclasping her rich, furred satin cloak, she threw it over the bodies of the Viceroy and Dahalia Santa Anna, thus shutting off the pitiful, gruesome, ghastly sight.

"We have come too late to save the child," said His Eminence sternly, "but not too late to avenge her."

Then pointing his finger at Iturbide he began—

"En nombre del Padre, y del Hijo, y del Espiritu Santo!"

"Stop!—" shrieked Madame de Iturbide, extending her hands in supplication. "Your Eminence will surely not place the ban of the Church upon my husband without a hearing?"

"What need of a hearing when the evidence of a foul crime lies unveiled before us?" murmured the Archbishop.

Iturbide rose with anger in his eyes.

"Proceed with the excommunication, your Eminence," he said, "only let the wrath of the Church of Rome descend upon the unworthy priest, the author of this night's work im-

132 Iturbide, A Soldier of Mexico.

prisoned in yonder secret passage of the Vice-roys."

"A priest—imprisoned in the secret passage of the Viceroys?" gasped His Eminence, starting back. "It is murder. For you know and I know that the passage was sealed at the farther end, by order of the Viceroy Calleja, the predecessor of Apodaca."

"And doubtless the accursed priest has discovered the fact by this time," replied Iturbide caustically.

"I demand that you tear down the secret panel with your troopers," cried His Eminence sternly. "Would you sacrifice another life in this accursed cause? Have you no heart?"

"There lies the heart of Iturbide," was the reply, as the Emperor pointed to Dahalia. "There lies my love, my future, my all. And there (pointing to the panel), there lies my revenge."

"But this is murder," gasped the Archbishop. "The murder of a Churchman and a member of our brotherhood. Refuse my demand and I shall withdraw from your cause the countenance and support of the Church of Rome."

"Go then," responded Iturbide, with a look of fierce defiance. "My cause was reared without the aid of the clergy, and it will live without the aid of the clergy. In England, Henry VIII. divorced Church and State. In France, the Republicans hurled defiance at the Pope. In Mexico, I, Agustin de Iturbide, Emperor by the Grace of God and the will of

Compliments of General Santa Anna. 133

the Mexican people, bid you go with your empty forms and mummery, fit alone for the priest-ridden Bourbons. For two hundred years the Church of Rome has preyed upon this poor country, like the sopilote of the desert, exercising the vilest extortions, practising the most fearful inhumanities, working upon the fears of the simple minded by the dread terrors of the Inquisition, and glutting the national resources to fatten your monks, your nuns, your cathedrals, and rear up a tinsel framework of ceremonials to pander to your idle vanities, while the ragged lepero, the beggared ranchero, and despairing tradesman bow their worn, emaciated bodies in the dust, to receive, in return for all they have given to the Church, the empty vacuous smile and meaningless benediction of some over-fed, lumbering priest, whose very shovel hat and black robe have been paid for from the full measure of their sacrifice. Yon man devil, who, I pray God, has already rendered his account, is an example of your sophistry, excusing all things on the ground that the end justifies the means."

"You have hurled down your grito of defiance and must answer to the Pope," cried the exasperated Archbishop, his form shaken with wrath. "The cause of the Excumulgado, has .ever been a lost cause."

"I shall answer to my God and to Him alone," cried Iturbide. "And if my cause fail because I have been the first of the Mexicans to raise my voice against extortionate priestcraft, then

134 Iturbide, A Soldier of Mexico.

be it so. But hearken, your Eminence, that day will come for Mexico when some man shall rise strong enough to forever divorce Church and State. Perhaps it may be an Iturbide— perhaps a man of a future generation—as yet unborn, but so surely as to-morrow's sun shall rise over the city, so surely will the hour and the man come. Go then, your Eminence, mete out the curses of the Church of Rome, let the Papal Bulls decry against my cause, flee across the water to the Court of the Bourbons. I defy you all and rest my cause before Almighty God."

The Archbishop raised his hand as though to pronounce the dread sentence of excommunication, but Madame de Iturbide cast herself before him and seized the hem of his robe.

"Forbear, your Eminence, I beseech you," she cried. "Grief has made my husband mad. He knows not what he says. He knows not what he does. I have ever been a faithful daughter of the Church and I will answer for my husband."

"So be it," said the Archbishop. "But until he retracts his words he rests under the ban of disapproval of the Church of Rome."

And motioning his suite to follow he passed with dignity from the scarlet chamber of the Viceroys, the suffragans chanting all the while.

CHAPTER XII.

THE COMPLIMENTS OF THE EMPEROR ITURBIDE.

THE Convent of Santa Teresa consisted of a retreat for about twenty nuns and a monastery of several hundred Jesuit Fathers. It was a large structure of quadrangular form, with a square court, enclosed by gloomy, forbidding-looking cloisters.

The Angelus was ringing, when a man and a woman, footsore and weary, with dirty, worn, tattered garments, knocked at the portals of the convent.

A voice from within spoke through the rega.

"Who knocks at the portals of Santa Teresa?"

The woman replied:

"A sister who desires sanctuary."

"Enter, little sister," said the same voice. And the wicket opened disclosing a number of thin, gaunt nuns, in great black robes, at the feet of the Mother Superior, and in the shadow, six blue-jacketed dragoons, headed by Captain Berdejo.

The Commander of the Jalapa troop advanced courteously, helmet in hand, and with a deferential bow said:

"We have anticipated your arrival by a few hours, lady la Garza,—and I have already per-

136 Iturbide, A Soldier of Mexico.

fected arrangements to carry out the sentence of death pronounced upon you by the Viceroy. The execution will take place at midnight. A pretty chase you have led us these many days,—through the mountains and over the lowlands. But all is well that ends well, and so, señora, I suppose you will want to spend the few hours left you at the Confessional."

The lady Juana la Garza looked with great, sorrowful eyes at the stern, uncompromising features of the Captain of the Blues, and in them saw no pity. Then at the sorrowful, sympathetic faces of the nuns.

Last at the passion-distorted face of Rafael Aristo, who trembling with a rage that deprived him of utterance, had fallen weakly against the wicket for support.

With a beautiful resignation, she turned gently to the priest and, bending close until their faces almost touched, she kissed him gently on the brow.

Then whispered softly in his ear:

" The Convent of Santa Teresa is but a few leagues from the hacienda of Mango de Clavo. If you can procure a swift horse, you can reach Santa Anna in time to save me. We have some few hours yet. If not—and you should fail—then tell him that my last—last thoughts were of him—tell him that perhaps it were better so—for I am all unworthy the love of such a man."

The face of the priest brightened.

With the light of new-found hope and joy in

Compliments of Emperor Iturbide. 137

his eyes, he bended over the lady's hand and then, before any one knew his intention, he vanished through the wicket and into the darkness of the night.

When he had gone the lady Juana la Garza turned to the Mother Superior and said very quietly :

" Mother, I am prepared to follow you."

And the Mother Superior, taking her hand, led her through the gloomy corridors of Santa Teresa, nuns and troopers following.

At an inn near the convent Rafael Aristo procured a horse and took the road to the south at a rapid gallop. Behind him along the northern road he heard the rumbling of heavy artillery wagons and the steady trot of cavalry, and surmised rightly that the army of the Emperor Iturbide was advancing from the Capitol. Ahead, however, the priest had a clear road and he urged his good steed to the utmost over the hard dry alkali road. As he sped along, he cast many a sidelong glance over the low-lying stretch of desert and wondered if his night-ride was destined to transform the peaceful waste into a charnel for the soldiers of Mexico, if the gentle chaparral was destined before morning to be crushed and bruised by the charge of cavalry and the rush of infantry, if Santa Anna's forces were sufficient in number to drive back the troopers of the Emperor and cut a way through to Santa Teresa, and if he, Rafael Aristo, was to see again in this life the

138 Iturbide, A Soldier of Mexico.

beautiful face of the woman he loved, Juana la Garza!

Again he urged his horse on, and on, and on, for the love of woman was his, than which man can have no greater incentive.

A turn of the road brought him to the outposts of Santa Anna's camp, and awakened him from his reverie. The click of a gunlock and the shrill challenge,—" Centinela alerta : " ringing out on the crisp air of the night, caused him to bring his steed to a standstill.

The camp stretched out in parallel lines for miles, the cavalry and infantry apart from the light artillery, which formed a separate division under General Marian, Santa Anna commanding the others.

Near the sentinel who barred his path, the priest saw a few old women making tortillas, while coffee-pots simmered over the camp-fires. The men of the outpost, big, strapping fellows, with bronzed, scarred cheeks, their heads covered by dirty, red handkerchiefs, or worn and tattered sombreros, their manta trousers supported by parti-colored bandas, from which protruded great pistols and machetes, lolled around smoking their cigarettes as though they had no other care in all the world.

" Pass me at once to the tent of the General Santa Anna, hombre—'tis a matter of life and death," panted the priest.

" Impossible, your reverence," replied the sentinel respectfully. " We have come by forced marches from Vera Cruz and officers and

Compliments of Emperor Iturbide. 139

men are exhausted. General Santa Anna has issued orders that no one disturb him to-night. You will have to rest here with us until morning and then, señor, if you wish you can see General Santa Anna."

With a deft swing of his arm Rafael Aristo pushed the sentinel out of the pathway and dashed on at full speed. The soldiers at the outpost shouted and followed, but did not fire, because their quarry was a son of the Church.

Rafael Aristo drew up his panting horse before a great tent, in front of which was planted Santa Anna's standard. Exhausted by his hard ride he flung himself to the ground and parted the flaps of the tent. The lights were burning low within, throwing weird, grotesque shadows on the flaps. A man, in the green and gold uniform of a brigadier, was seated at a table on which was a great war map which he had evidently been studying, but his head had fallen upon his arm and he slept.

The abrupt entrance of the priest awakened him and he sprang to his feet, his hand upon his sword-hilt. The face which met the eager gaze of Rafael Aristo had once been a very handsome face, but it was deeply lined and haggard from battles, forced marches and all-night vigils. The heavy jet-black curls were streaked with silver threads, giving the daring General a dignity which well became him. The eyes were weary, tired-looking eyes yet in the dim candle-light they threw out a scintillat-

140 Iturbide, A Soldier of Mexico.

ing glitter that fascinated the priest as no other eyes had ever done in all his life. He saw now why the lady Juana la Garza loved this magnetic, soldier gentleman, the idol of the Southland.

"My orders——" began General Santa Anna imperiously.

"Excellency—the lady Juana la Garza—Convent of Santa Teresa—execution—midnight——" panted the priest and fell in a dead faint to the ground.

Without waiting for the priest to recover himself Santa Anna rushed hastily from his tent and crossed over to that of Colonel Duran adjoining. A number of brilliantly uniformed staff officers were carousing and making merry over their wine. Deep silence fell as the General entered and stood regarding them, a drawn sword in his hand, his face calm, impassive. Every man set down his glass and stood at attention.

"Colonel Duran, you will advance your regiment and take the enemy upon the right," began Santa Anna hurriedly.

"To-night——?" gasped Colonel Duran.

"To-night—at once," said Santa Anna incisively.

General Marian broke in—

"The enemy are fortified on the Santa Teresa road. My vedette Captain reports that they outnumber us five to one. Even with our reserves, which will not arrive until five o'clock to-morrow morning, the ·Emperor has an ad-

Compliments of Emperor Iturbide. 141

vantage in men and position. It is madness to think of an advance to-night."

General Santa Anna turned to an orderly.

" Teniente, have my cavalry ready to move in ten minutes."

The Teniente saluted and left the tent at once. A moment later a bugle sounded the call " boots and saddles."

Santa Anna turned again to his astonished officers.

" I see you are not in accord with me," he said pleasantly, " I breakfast to-morrow morning in the Convent of Santa Teresa, gentlemen."

" In all probability we'll breakfast in hell," growled Colonel Duran.

" Perhaps," smiled Santa Anna, and his eyes gleamed luridly with the fire of battle. " But we'll have distinguished company, gentlemen, for in half an hour we will join battle with the enemy. I will lead the cavalry attack upon the enemy's center, Colonel Duran the infantry upon the enemy's right and you, General Marian, will bring your batteries in play upon the enemy's left and concentrate your fire to draw his attention from the center which I mean to force to-night."

" Impossible——" began Duran.

" There is no such word for Santa Anna," smiled that General. " We rendezvous after the battle at Santa Teresa, gentlemen. God speed you all, and speed our battle-cry, Mexico and Santa Anna."

As they echoed the viva of their chief, Santa

142 Iturbide, A Soldier of Mexico.

Anna bowed very cordially and passed out to where his troopers waited him. With a set face and lips tightly compressed Santa Anna vaulted into his saddle and led his band forward at a rapid trot. He had thought the woman he loved was safe and awaiting him in the care of the priest who had saved her. For love of her he had raised the standard of revolt and declared against the Emperor, for love of her he had abandoned the impregnable fortress of San Juan de Uloa and led his little army to the north that he might cut his way victorious into the Capitol and make her the first lady of Mexico. And to-night, on the eve of his success, when his picked reserves were almost at hand, the news of her peril forced his hand and gave him an almost insurmountable task.

" By God, I'll drive them back, I'll drive them back," he muttered, " I'll drive them back if it costs me every man I have."

And Santa Anna led his troopers on with increased speed.

Meanwhile the camp was all confusion. The vedettes had been called in and the infantry of Colonel Duran and the field batteries of General Marian began their advance to certain destruction. Every officer of Santa Anna's staff knew what odds confronted them. But Santa Anna had trained his men to obey without question and cheerily they followed their fearless leader, though they knew it was for many of them the last battle, though they feared that

Compliments of Emperor Iturbide. 143

the morning's sun would rise for them no more, for Santa Anna led them on, and with Santa Anna they could smile at the very gates of hell.

In the tent of General Santa Anna, the lights were burning low, when the priest Rafael Aristo came to himself. A great crucifix was hung on one of the flaps of the tent and the priest prostrated himself before it, praying for the lady Juana la Garza whose life hung by a thread.

Outside was the clatter of cavalry, the deep heavy tread of infantry which gradually died away in the distance. Then the sound of the heavy gun-carriages of General Marian as battery after battery passed. Rafael Aristo listened to the shouting of the drivers as they lashed their horses and then continued his prayer. Far away in the distance sounded the rattle and crash of musketry, and the resonant booming of field-guns, but above all the frenzied cries of men in the agony of mortal conflict. The priest sprang to his feet and listened with clasped hands, then moved by a sudden inspiration he seized the great crucifix and rushed from the tent in time to join the last battery as it swept on to action and death, the swarth artillery-men shouting their battle-cry, " Mexico and Santa Anna!" and the priest, waving the crucifix and echoing their cry, " Mexico and Santa Anna!" sprang upon an axletree seat and was swept along in the charge.

The nuns of Santa Teresa were at the re-

144 Iturbide, A Soldier of Mexico.

fectory. This, like the cells, was a gloomy apartment, so furnished as to be a constant picture of the mutability of human life. Upon the walls at stated intervals were suspended the moldy bones of divers Saints. In the center of the table was a skull and crossbones. While the twenty nuns supped of their simple fare, consisting of an apple and a tortilla for each, the Mother Superior read aloud the prayers of the Church of Rome.

Apart from the rest the condemned woman listened and waited the coming of the Father Confessor.

The hour was eleven.

One hour of life.

Would Santa Anna reach her in time to save her?

From an adjoining room came the voices of Captain Berdejo's troopers toasting each other over their wine. Soldier-like they had no thought of the poor soul so soon to be hurried into eternity.

There was the sound of chanting and the great rumbling wheels of a coach from the courtyard.

"It is the good Padre Madrid," said the Mother Superior to the condemned woman. "Little sister, art thou prepared for the Confessional?"

The bell of the convent tolled mournfully the quarter.

"I am prepared for the Confessional," echoed the lady Juana la Garza, listlessly.

Compliments of Emperor Iturbide.   145

There was still three-quarters of an hour left.

And the lady Juana la Garza believed in her lover.

"Come, then," said the Mother Superior, taking her hand. And she led her from the refectory out through the gloomy cloister to the Confessional.

A gorgeously-attired priest, in violet robe, with a scarlet cloak, knelt prostrate before a huge wooden crucifix, chanting the prayers of the Church of Rome.

" Padre Madrid, I bring thee the condemned woman, that her last moments may be spent in preparation to meet her God."

The priest bowed and continued his chanting.

The Mother Superior withdrew, crossing herself.

The lady Juana la Garza sank upon her knees, and began telling her rosary. All hope had left her now. With a white, wan face, she looked pitifully at the great crucifix, before which the priest still knelt.

" Juana——" murmured the priest.

The lady la Garza pressed her hand to her heart and gasped :

" Madre de Dios—Antonio——"

" Yes, Antonio !" replied the priest passionately, and turned suddenly upon her, holding out his arms.

" Antonio, who loves you with all the love that his broken heart has left; Antonio, who,

10

146 Iturbide, A Soldier of Mexico.

loving you, has come to die for you, or failing that has come to die with you."

And he would have embraced her.

But with a great cry of awful agony, she shrank from him.

" Ah, God—you are bleeding—you are wounded—Antonio, my Antonio———" she sobbed piteously.

" Yes, I had to cut my way through the army of Iturbide, which was advancing upon Mango de Clavo. To-morrow I should have given him battle—for I have raised the grito of revolt against the man who took my little sister's honor. And I think I should have won the day, for my reserves were advancing from the south. But when, to-night, your messenger came to me and told me of your impending fate, I started with what forces I could gather, and advanced upon mine enemy. Ah, God ! it was a battle—and we cut our way through,—but of my brave Jorochos, there are scarce half a hundred left. And Iturbide is in hot pursuit. My men hold the only approach to the convent, and will hold it against all the army of Iturbide, until every man of them has fallen. Fate sent the Padre Madrid across our path, in his great coach, scarce half an hour since. He was bearing the Host to the dying. Around his carriage ran six acolytes in robes of white, chanting and waving their incense. We waylaid them and slew the Confessor and the boys. Then, donning their robes, myself and six of my most trusted men gained access

Compliments of Emperor Iturbide. 147

to the convent. My companions hold the approaches to the Confessional."

"Ah, Dios—you do love me—you do indeed love me——" sobbed the lady Juana la Garza, throwing herself into his outstretched arms. "And since we cannot live together, we can at least die together."

"Talk not of death while Santa Anna has his sword to defend you," said her lover.

And throwing off the robes of the Father Confessor, he drew his saber, and stood before her, every inch a soldier, in his blood-bespattered uniform of green and gold.

"Come—my love—my niña—there is still time and I will lead you to liberty and to love——"

Solemnly rang through the Confessional the first stroke of twelve.

"Ah, Dios—too late—too late——" gasped the lady Juana la Garza.

As if to verify her words, the furious clash of sabers rang through the corridor.

With the light of battle in his eyes, Santa Anna gently disengaged her clinging arms, and with a passionate kiss of farewell, cried:

"Wait you here, my darling. If I live, I will return to you and lead you from this hotbed of danger."

And then he sprang into the corridor, where his brave troopers were fighting the soldiers of Captain Berdejo. Slowly the soldiers of the Blues retreated before the determined onset of Santa Anna and his Jorocho cavalrymen. And

148 Iturbide, A Soldier of Mexico.

retreating, entered the room where Berdejo had made merry with his officers but a short time since. And now there were but three of all the combatants left alive—Santa Anna—and opposed to him, the Captain and Lieutenant of the Blues. And Berdejo, supported with his left arm, the body of a boy sergeant, which he used as a buckler in this awful game of life and death.

For his sword had already crossed the sword of Santa Anna, and he knew that he had found his master. For Santa Anna was the best swordsman in Mexico.

The room was small and there was little opportunity to display any great maneuvering. Round and round the apartment swayed the three combatants, and Santa Anna allowed the blades of his opponents, to play along his own, keeping his eyes fixed upon the Lieutenant, a huge massive man with a great black beard.

There was time for the Captain later.

And the Lieutenant pressed Santa Anna the more fiercely, since in the eyes of Santa Anna he read death. Once he made a pass at Santa Anna's head, but missed his stroke and the point of his saber struck the partition. And Santa Anna returned the pass and by the soft feel of resistance to his point, knew that he had pierced the Lieutenant's shoulder.

With an awful oath the Lieutenant dropped his saber and sank weakly against the wall.

And Captain Berdejo, making a fierce rush upon Santa Anna, fought as only a desperate

Slowly the soldiers of the Blues retreated before the determined onset of Santa Anna. * * *
Page 148.

Compliments of Emperor Iturbide. 149

man can, and fighting, broke his opponent's saber.

But Santa Anna grasped the heavy wine bottle from the table hard by and, with the cool desperation of a man who sees nothing but death before him, hurled it at his opponent's head, felling him like an ox.

Then with a savage cry of joy, he would have turned again to the corridor, to rejoin his love, but as he faced the door, he saw standing there, surrounded by his brilliantly uniformed staff, the man he most hated in all the world—Iturbide.

"Buenos noches, General Santa Anna," said the Emperor smiling. "It seems we have arrived a little late to participate in this drama." General Antonio Lopez de Santa Anna, leaned weakly against the table, and gazed with lackluster eyes at the man who had robbed him of his sister, who had defeated his faithful Jorochos, and who was now about to crown his triumph by sending the woman he loved to her death, for it was not reasonable to suppose that a hardened soldier like the Emperor Iturbide would have any consideration for the man who had sought to bring about the downfall of the Empire, nor for the woman he loved.

"You have just five minutes to live," continued Iturbide in a stern voice. "You have dared to raise the grito of revolt against the man who was your Emperor—God's anointed —the Liberator of Mexico."

"And the man who dishonored the little

150 Iturbide, A Soldier of Mexico.

sister I entrusted to his care," added Santa Anna, with an awful look of agony and a great sadness in his voice.

Iturbide started as though he had received a blow,—advanced upon Santa Anna, with features hard and set. Then controlling himself, with an effort said :

" General Santa Anna, I swear as God is my judge, that Dahalia's honor was sacred to me. Religiously I kept the trust imposed upon me. I loved her—ah God,—I loved her better than life itself. And when she was taken from me, my heart was broken. While your sister lived I could never forget that I was a gentleman of Mexico, and her honor was dearer to me than mine own."

" You swear that this is the truth as God is your judge?" said Santa Anna, rising to his feet with a radiant look of joy upon his face.

" As God is my judge, I swear that this is the truth," said Iturbide, raising his hand to heaven.

" 'Tis all that I could ask," cried Santa Anna. " And I thank the good God that He permits me to go to my death with the knowledge that the little sister I loved was pure."

Iturbide held out his hand. But Santa Anna sadly shook his head.

" No—no," he said finally. " I am no hypocrite. I raised the grito of revolt against you when I saw that you had driven out the Spanish Viceroys only to create a New World Empire for yourself. I am a Mexican of the

Compliments of Emperor Iturbide. 151

Mexicans, and were I freed to-night, I should rally my scattered troopers against you to-morrow, and do my best to tear down the throne you have mounted."

"For Dahalia's sake I would have wished it otherwise," said Iturbide, regretfully. "But you pronounce your own death sentence, when you declare against me. If I would have peace in Mexico, I must crush out mine enemies. We might have been friends."

"Yes—the Liberator-General and Santa Anna might have been friends," was the reply. "But the Emperor of Mexico and Santa Anna —never. So order your soldiers to proceed with the execution, Excellency, I am ready."

And he threw back his head proudly and folded his arms upon his blood-stained breast.

Iturbide motioned to a squad of soldiers in the corridor and they took their position before the condemned man, while the Emperor and his staff moved aside.

At a word from the officer in charge they slowly raised their muskets.

Before the fatal word of command could be given, a pale, sorrowful-looking woman, with disheveled hair, and grief-stricken features, rushed into the room and threw her arms around Santa Anna.

"Ah, Dios—Juana—my darling"— groaned Santa Anna—"I could have died like a soldier but now—now I am all unmanned. Why have you come here when you might have escaped your enemies?"

152 Iturbide, A Soldier of Mexico.

"I have come to die with the man I loved," sobbed the woman, clinging passionately to him and twining her soft arms around his neck.

Iturbide turned towards them and in a kindly, gentle tone said:

"We are not butchers of women, my lady. Nor is a military execution a fitting sight for your eyes. So if you will leave us——"

"Leave the man I love—the man who is about to die, because he risked his all for me?" gasped the lady Juana la Garza. "Ah, no, no, no! If we cannot live together, we can at least die together. Grant me this one request, Excellency. I am a Mexican woman and I have asked no mercy for Santa Anna nor for myself. I too know how to die, and my one great desire is to be permitted to die in the arms of the man I love."

Gently Santa Anna disengaged her clasp, and advancing to the Emperor held out his hand.

"A few moments ago, I refused your offer of friendship, because, as a Republican at heart, I could not tolerate a Mexican Emperor. But you have offered life and liberty to the one woman in all the world to me. I thank you. I staked my all in this game of life and death and I have lost. I am ready to pay the reckoning. Have the lady Juana la Garza removed and let the execution proceed."

And with a great effort he turned his back upon her.

She fell upon her knees before the Emperor

Compliments of Emperor Iturbide. 153

Iturbide, and seizing his hand, sobbed piteously.

"Ah, Excellency—do not let them take me from him—let us die together—it is all I ask—it is all I ask."

And she fainted.

Gently they bore her from the room and Santa Anna turned to Iturbide with an inclination of the head, saying softly:

"I thank your Excellency."

Iturbide looked at him with admiration, and looking saw upon his face the look of the dead Dahalia,—the look of the little woman who had drank of the death potion intended for her Emperor.

And seeing the likeness of the dead sister in the living brother, his heart was heavy with grief and he groaned:

"Ah, no, no,—I cannot do it—I cannot do it.— Dahalia pleads with me to spare you. Perhaps I am preparing the downfall of the Empire I have builded—perhaps I am setting free the man who will foment rebellion and civil war in Mexico. But for her sake I will take the chance. General Antonio Lopez de Santa Anna, you are free—free to depart with the woman you love."

Santa Anna grasped Iturbide's hand and gently raised it to his lips.

"Again I thank your Excellency," he said, "but I am in duty-bound, as a gentleman of Mexico, to tell you that, when I return to the Southland, my first act will be to rally to my

154 Iturbide, A Soldier of Mexico.

banners the remnant of my army, and to declare against the Empire, since dearer to Santa Anna than his life and even his love is Mexico, his country. Yet perhaps may come that time when opportunity will be given to General Antonio Lopez de Santa Anna to remember that the Emperor Iturbide gave him his life and his love, and he will not forget."

For answer the Emperor pointed to the door.

And Santa Anna passed through the brilliantly-uniformed suite of officers—to liberty— and to the woman he loved.

EPILOGUE.

A.

A NEW moon broke through the nebulosity of the southern sky and cast its gentle, yellow light upon the long, low stretch of alkali desert.

The silence of the night prevailed unbroken.

To the north, out of the low-lying mist which hovered like a dense pall over the lowlands, petrous Popocatapetl and Iztaccihuatl,—gruesome, gray phantasms of the night—loomed out of the darkness.

Through the veil of mist, in the south, a paraselene sky caught out of the great desert the shades of the waning night, alternating with fitful, phosphorescent strands of green and gold, orange and vermilion, in the east,—heralds of the dawning day.

As the gray of early morning slowly drove back the blackish gloom, amorphous shadows of the night became tangible realities of the day, and far as eye could see was one huge conglutination of human bodies, horses and ordnance.

In the glister of the fine white alkali, was gluey red crassament which had formed a thick viscous pool.

Under the battered flanges of a field-gun, a

156 Iturbide, A Soldier of Mexico.

group of fierce Jorochos were sleeping their last sleep, their faces ghastly, drawn, their jaws fallen, their teeth gleaming white, their mutilated bodies drenched in the fluxion of their own blood. The bronzed, ugly faces with contracted foreheads, beady, bulging eyes, high cheekbones and square, massive animal jaws, were not pleasant to look upon in death.

Near them, blood-soaked, lay a troop of the Emperor's dragoons, under and alongside the stiffening bodies of their horses,—riders and steeds shot down in the charge by the last fire from the Jorocho battery, which had finally succumbed to superior numbers, but had surrendered only to King Death.

Between the two groups and beside a great wooden crucifix lay a squat, pitiful figure, in the long, black robe of a Jesuit father. The position of the priest indicated that he had been in command of the Jorocho battery, and he had evidently been cut down by the charging dragoons when rallying his men around the cross of Christ. There was a great gash across the man's forehead, from which a little red stream had trickled over his ecchymotic face, forming a dark red congelation. The body of a dapple-gray cavalry horse had fallen across the man's left arm, breaking it at the bend of the elbow.

Through the mist broke the red blaze of the rising sun, and lighted the gruesome repast of the Sopilotes, great black scavengers, who foraged from body to body with a jubilant,

Epilogue. 157

" Caw, caw, caw—caw, caw, caw," plucking and tearing at the soft, yielding flesh of their silent prey, and holding the quivering red tid-bits aloft in blood-reddened claws, while they drove their sharp, razor-like beaks into eye or cheek to further glut and gorge their carrion-swelled bodies. And so from group to group, from rebel Jorocho to royal dragoon, went the carrion vultures, performing well their gruesome task, and leaving, instead of the bronzed, battle-scarred faces, smooth, eburnean, white, grinning skulls shining in the sunlight of the early morning. And so from group to group went the carrion vultures, until they came at last to the blood-shrouded group under the battered flanges of the field gun.

The sudden descent of the carrion vultures startled from under the body of the priest a huge rattlesnake, which, rearing itself from the encrimsoned pool where it had lain, coiled itself as though for a spring, hissing angrily all the while, then sullenly glided off to a more quiet retreat near some neighboring cacti. Likewise fled from the stark and silent dead a body of red ants which had been attracted to the group by the putrescent effluvium given off from the bodies already beginning to rot in the sunlight.

One huge, black vulture, so swollen from carnal repast as to make his movements clumsy, settled heavily on the head of the priest and began to peck slowly at the gash upon the forehead, whereupon the blood began to trickle

158 Iturbide, A Soldier of Mexico.

afresh down the ecchymotic, swollen face. A nervous tremor shook the body of the priest and the muscles of his face worked convulsively. Something between a sob and a hiccough came from the prostrate form, and a red-white foam flecked the blanched lips. The huge carrion vulture sank a great claw into the priest's right eye, tearing the ball and crushing it back into the socket.

With an awful groan and a sob the priest raised his right arm, and the carrion bird of prey flapped its great black wings, essaying to fly, but, overweighted by its glut of blood and flesh, it toppled down and off the swollen face, and the right hand of the pain-maddened man closed around the great black neck, and crushed and ground and tore, until the hand retained in its fierce clasp only a soft, pulpy mass of quivering flesh and warm red blood,

Sobbing and hiccoughing, the priest shook off the slimy, oozy, pulpy mass, and with an effort carried his right hand, blood-soaked and gluey wet, to the maimed, sightless eyeball, which burned and ached and bled, and did more to bring the man to consciousness by the very exquisite pang of pain than aught else could have done. He attempted to raise himself upon his elbow, but the body of the dapple-gray held his limp left arm immobile. He exerted himself, more by instinct than by any consciousness of what he was doing, to release the injured limb from the vise which held it down. It yielded a little, but the effort gave

Epilogue. 159

him a thrill of awful agony and he shrieked aloud. Again he sought to release the arm from the sickening weight which held it, and this time succeeded, but from very agony fell back weak and fainting. For a long time he lay silent, his body quivering from an occasional hiccoughing.

When at last he came again to himself the sun was a fiery ball of red directly overhead, and its fierce heat beat upon his unprotected head, overpowering his reason with frenetic scotomy. He essayed to rise, but paraplegy held him powerless for a long time. He seemed no longer a human being, but a bloody, raging, nameless thing.

Again and again he essayed to rise and again and again fell back.

"God Almighty!—God Almighty!—God Almighty!" he cried again and again.

After awhile he dragged himself with an effort a few paces to where the blood-red crucifix lay in the white alkali of the desert. He caught the crucifix to him and kissed it again and again, babbling all the while in his delirium— babbling of the Church, babbling of Mexico, babbling of the woman he loved.

He was quite mad, poor priest; crazed by the pitiless heat which seethed from the caldron overhead; crazed by the pain in his sightless, pulpy eye; crazed by the parched, swollen lips and the dried, parchment-like tongue which protruded from his mouth, a shapeless red thing like a piece of dried leather.

160 Iturbide, A Soldier of Mexico.

With his uninjured eye he made out the still bleeding, bruised body of the carrion bird of prey, and caught it up with his right hand, squeezing out the viscous red ooze upon his parched lips and tongue, and drawing in the nauseous effluence with little chuckling gasps of glee. At last, when he had finished his loathsome draught, he flung the shapeless thing from him and looked long and earnestly to the north. Nothing met his eye but the corse-strewn stretch of alkali, with its covering of dead dragoons, dead Jorochos, dead horses and broken gun carriages.

Everything was still and silent, on every side, save the feasting sopilotes, circling here and there with incessant, rancorous,

"Caw, caw, caw,—caw, caw, caw."

He turned himself with an effort to the south, and looked long into vacancy, scanning the desert from zenith to horizon, but no single living thing except the sopilotes could be seen, and he groaned aloud with an awful sense of loneliness and abandonment. Nearer sounded the never-ceasing,

"Caw, caw, caw,—caw, caw, caw,"

and the priest shuddered as he thought of the shapeless dead thing whose blood he had drained.

Gradually came to him a fixed idea, which began to shape itself into words, and he murmured over and over again:

"She is there, — she is there, — she is there——"

Epilogue. 161

Then after a while:

"God Almighty, good God, merciful God Almighty,—give me strength to see her once—once again before I die."

And with an almost superhuman effort, his swollen lips compressed, his jaw firmly set, he began to drag himself with his right arm over the silent hillocks of the dead, towards the south, babbling all the while.

162 Iturbide, A Soldier of Mexico.

EPILOGUE.

B.

A BEAUTIFUL woman in a stylish riding-habit, mounted upon a dapple gray, and a soldierly-looking, handsome man, in a uniform of green and gold, upon a great war-horse, were riding upon that part of the road to Vera Cruz, lying to the north.

Twilight was just setting in as they drew near the hacienda of Mango de Clavo,—the hereditary estate of the Santa Annas. The soil was rich and fertile,—great herds of fat, sleek-looking cattle browsed through the pasturage and tropical undergrowth, while wiry, well-groomed horses, startled at the approach of the intruders, would dash through the forest and along the shores of the gulf, pursued by the bronzed vacqueros whose care it was to watch them.

As the evening drew on, they began to pass the large granaries and storehouses of the estate. Exterior to these was a huge fortified wall, garrisoned by armed retainers. Near the granaries were a few jacals, around which stood the Zaragates and Gauchinangos, or peon retainers, who rent the air with cries of joy at their beloved master's homecoming.

At last the master of Mango de Clavo and

Epilogue. 163

his fair companion came to the great drive-
way, leading to the mansion house, the whole
length of which, on either side, was lined with
Jorocho cavalrymen—bronzed, intrepid, wiry,
wild-eyed little men, who seldom slept. For
they were the Cossack lancers of the South,
who in the thick of battle were on and off
their horses, now thrusting with their lances,
now performing miracles of sharpshooting,
with their carbines, now wading over the blood-
stained batteries they had swept aside like
chaff, to perform new wonders in the resistless
rush against the enemy.

And so, on this particular evening, when
they had assembled to greet their chieftain,
General Antonio Lopez de Santa Anna, and
the woman for love of whom he had sacrificed
his chosen ones, their impatient ponies pawed
the ground, to the accompaniment of their silver trappings, and the little group of fierce,
savage-looking officers, sat like marionettes in
their saddles—behind them the fierce Jorochos,
every lance at an angle, every carbine across
the crupper, every bearskin shako jauntily set,
every bristling pair of mustaches stiffened with
pride.

And as he saw once more the devoted band,
which he had thought lost to him forever, a
feeling of sadness came upon Santa Anna, and
there was moisture in his eyes. But as he
looked at the beautiful woman at his side, his
grief gave way to happiness, and he told himself that for the love of such a woman he would

164 Iturbide, A Soldier of Mexico.

send this remnant of his dear army to the gates of hell.

And when they had come to the great mansion, General Santa Anna took his lady's hand, and after assisting her to dismount, led her into the patio of Mango de Clavo, where a great banquet was spread for the homecoming of master and mistress.

The dinner was a most elaborate one. Olla podrida in great silver bowls, juicy tender joints on platters of Dresden china, steaming chili con carne, dainty entrées, freshest of pineapples, and strawberries from the plantation, interspersed with wines rich and varied, and followed by coffee and cigarros.

And when the toasts were drunk, Santa Anna, looking at the gallant officers around the festal board proposed :

"The most beautiful lady in all the land!"

And the officers with their eyes upon the lady Juana la Garza echoed right heartily :

"The most beautiful lady in all the land!"

And the night wore on apace—a night of feasting and revelry. And on the stroke of twelve appeared in the doorway two dust-bespattered troopers, supporting between them an abject, gaunt, pitiful-looking figure, in a black cassock, a great cut upon his forehead, and the ashen hue of death upon his face, his right eye a sightless pulp, his left arm limp and helpless by his side, a figure more thing than man.

The priest Rafael Aristo!

Epilogue. 165

Through the startled group of officers they led him, and never paused until they had set him gently in a chair near General Santa Anna.

" Rafael Aristo ! " gasped the lady Juana la Garza.

" Yes—Rafael—Aristo "— said the priest with a great effort—" Rafael Aristo,—who was left last night for dead upon the battlefield. But a merciful God—gave me strength—to live —to look once more upon the one woman—in all the world—to me—and to know that she will be happy. I have dragged my poor, maimed body—along the alkali desert, all this day,— until these faithful ones—found me. Something told me that my mission had not been— fruitless—that Santa Anna would be in time— and I—I could not bear to die—my children— without giving you—the blessing of the Church of Rome. That blessing I now pronounce— upon this man and this woman—for I am once more a priest of the Holy Church—and I think the good God will pardon me—if I was mistaken in seeking what other men have sought —I think He will pardon me, I say—because I have given my life—that the woman I loved might live—and be happy—and be happy— ah God—I am coming—I am coming—the Church—the Church of Rome—Mexico."

His head fell back ; a great stream of blood issued from his lips and so he died.

And the lady Juana la Garza, kneeling beside him, pressed a gentle kiss upon the pallid, death-dampened brow.

Then turning, saw her lover standing near, and throwing herself into his outstretched arms, buried her face upon his great chest and wept like a little child.

TWENTIETH EDITION.

SOME PUBLICATIONS OF THE

May be obtained through any bookseller, or will be mailed postpaid, on receipt of the published price.

A DESCRIPTIVE AND ALPHABETICALLY ARRANGED LIST OF MINERALS, PRECIOUS AND OTHER STONES. By Felix J. Troughton. Twenty-five Cents.

ADVERTISING AGENTS' DIRECTORY, THE. Cloth. One Dollar. (In preparation.)

AFLOAT WITH OLD GLORY. By H. V. Warren. Cloth, 12mo. One Dollar.

AMERICAN ELOQUENCE. A Selection of Orations. By Carlos Martyn. (In preparation.)

AMERICAN WOMEN OF THE TIME. Revised to date and edited by Mr. Charles F. Rideal, Mrs. John King Van Rensselaer and Dr. Carlos Martyn. Cloth. $7.50. (In preparation.)

ARICKAREE TREASURE, THE. By Albert G. Clarke, Jr. Cloth, 12mo. One Dollar.

AT THE TEMPLE GATES. By Stewart Doubleday. Cloth, 12mo. One Dollar.

AUNT LUCY'S CABIN. By June Kankakee. Cloth. Daintily produced. Fifty Cents.

BALLADS OF BROTHERHOOD. By Alphonso Alva Hopkins. Cloth, small 12mo, 84 pages. Fifty Cents.

BEAUTIFUL HAND OF THE DEVIL, THE. By Margaret Hobson. Cloth, small 12mo. Fifty Cents.

BIRDS UNCAGED AND OTHER POEMS. By Burton L. Collins. Cloth, 12mo. One Dollar.

BITS OF SUNSHINE. By Clarence L. Miller. Cloth, 12mo. One Dollar.

BOBTAIL DIXIE. By Abbie N. Smith. Cloth, 12mo. Illustrated. One Dollar.

BOOK PUBLISHERS' DIRECTORY, THE. Cloth. One Dollar. (In preparation.)

BRITANNIA; OR, THE WHITE QUEEN. By the Rev. South G. Preston. Cloth, 12mo. One Dollar.

BY THEIR FRUITS. By Edith M. Nicholl. Cloth, 12mo. One Dollar.

CANDLE LIGHT, A, AND OTHER POEMS. By Louis Smirnow. Illustrated. Cloth. One Dollar.

CAT TALES IN VERSE. By Elliott Walker. Cloth, with cover designed by C. H. Rowe. Fifty Cents.

CAVALIER POETS. By Clarence M. Lindsay. Cloth, small 12mo. Fifty Cents.

CHARLES DICKENS' HEROINES AND WOMEN FOLK. By Charles F. Rideal. With two drawings by Florence Pash. Cloth. Fifty Cents.

CHIEFS OF CAMBRIA, THE. By Morgan P. Jones. Cloth, 12mo, $1.25.

CHRISTIAN SCIENCE AND KINDRED SUPERSTITIONS. By the Rev. Charles F. Winbigler. Cloth, 12mo. One Dollar.

ABBEY PRESS, 114 Fifth Ave., New York.

SOME PUBLICATIONS OF THE

CHRIST'S MESSAGE TO THE CHURCHES. By William M. Campbell. Cloth, 12mo, 170 pages. One Dollar.

CITY BOYS' LIFE IN THE COUNTRY; OR, HOWARD AND WESTON AT BEDFORD. By Clinton Osgood Burling. Cloth, 12mo. Illustrated. One Dollar.

COALS OF FIRE. By M. Frances Hanford Delanoy. Cloth, 12mo. One Dollar.

CONCHITA'S ANGELS. By Agnes Camplejohn Pritchard. Cloth, 12mo, 216 pages. One Dollar.

CONSPIRACY OF YESTERDAY, A. By Mical Ui Niall. Cloth, 12mo, daintily produced, 75 pages. Fifty Cents.

CONTINENTAL CAVALIER, A. By Kimball Scribner. Cloth, 12mo. Illustrated, 258 pages. One Dollar.

CORDELIA AND OTHER POEMS. By N. B. Ripley. Cloth, small 12mo. Fifty Cents.

COUNCIL OF THREE, THE. By Charles A. Seltzer. Cloth, 12mo, 177 pages. One Dollar.

COUNTRY STORE WINDOW, A. By Herbert Holmes. Cloth, 12mo. One Dollar.

CRICKET ON THE HEARTH, THE. By Charles Dickens. Fully illustrated. Dainty edition.. 12mo. One Dollar.

CRIME OF CHRISTENDOM, THE. By Daniel Seelye Gregory, L.D., LL.D. Cloth, 12mo, 330 pages. $1.50.

CROSS OF HONOR, THE. By Charles F. Rideal and C. Gordon Winter. Second Edition. One Dollar.

CULTURE FROM READING. A book for everybody. By Albert R. Alexander. Twenty-five Cents.

CUPID IN GRANDMA'S GARDEN. By Mrs. David O. Paige. Illustrated. Fifty Cents.

CURIOUS CASE OF GENERAL DELANEY SMYTHE, THE. By W. H. Gardner, Lieutenant-Colonel U. S. A. (retired). Cloth, 12mo. Illustrated, 204 pages. One Dollar.

DANGER SIGNALS FOR NEW CENTURY MANHOOD. By Edward A. Tabor. 12mo, cloth bound, 316 pages. One Dollar.

DAUGHTER OF THE PROPHETS, A. By Curtis Van Dyke. Cloth, 12mo. One Dollar.

DAYS THAT ARE NO MORE, THE. By Elizabeth Bryant Johnston. Cloth, 12mo. One Dollar.

DEFEATED, BUT VICTOR STILL. By William V. Lawrence. Cloth, 12mo, 424 pages. One Dollar.

DEMOCRACY AND THE TRUSTS. By Edwin B. Jennings. Cloth, 65 pages. Fifty Cents.

DEVIL'S DIARY, THE. By Louis M. Elshemus. Cloth, 12mo. One Dollar. Paper, Fifty Cents.

DEVOUT BLUEBEARD, A. By Marie Graham. Cloth, 12mo, 300 pages. One Dollar.

DIABOLICAL IN SCRIPTURE AND IN HUMAN LIFE, THE. By Harold Stormbrow, D.D., LL.D. Cloth, 8vo, limited edition. Ten Dollars. (In preparation.)

DID SHE FAIL? By Anna Fielding. Cloth, small 12mo, neatly bound. Fifty Cents.

DIP IN THE POOL, A.—(Bethesda.) By Barnetta Brown. Cloth (Miniature), daintily produced. Twenty-five Cents.

DIRECTORY OF MEDICAL WOMEN, THE. Cloth. $1.50. (In preparation.)

DOCTOR JOSEPHINE. By Willis Barnes. Cloth, 12mo. One Dollar.

DOCTRINES OF THE BOOK OF ACTS, THE. By G. L. Young. Cloth, 12mo. One Dollar.

ABBEY PRESS, 114 Fifth Ave., New York.

SOME PUBLICATIONS OF THE

DOLINDA AND THE TWINS. By Dora Harvey Munyon, A.M. Cloth, 12mo. Illustrated. Seventy-five Cents.

DOOMED TURK, THE; OR, THE END OF THE EASTERN QUESTION. By E. Middleton. Cloth. Fifty Cents.

EGYPTIAN RING, THE. By Nellie Tolman Sawyer. Cloth, small 12mo. Fifty Cents.

EVERYDAY CHILDREN. By May C. Emmel. Cloth. Fifty Cents.

EXPERIENCE. "How to Take It: How to Make It." By Barnetta Brown. Cloth (Miniature), daintily produced. Twenty-five Cents.

FEATHER'S WEIGHT, A. By Amarala Martin. Cloth, small 12mo, 131 pages. Fifty Cents.

FIGHTING AGAINST FATE. By Moses D. Morris. Cloth, 12mo, 275 pages, with one hundred illustrations. One Dollar.

FLOWER OF THE TROPICS, A, AND OTHER STORIES OF MEXICO AND THE BORDER. By Warner P. Sutton. Cloth, 12mo, 121 pages, daintily printed and bound. One Dollar.

FOOTSTEPS OF TRUTH. By I. M. Morris. Cloth, 12mo. One Dollar.

FOUNDATION RITES. By Lewis Dayton Burdick. Cloth, 12mo. $1.50.

FRENCH-ENGLISH AND ENGLISH-FRENCH PRONOUNCING DICTIONARY on the basis of Nugent, with many new words in general use exhibiting the pronunciation of all French words in pure English sounds, and giving the parts of speech, and gender of French nouns. By a member of the University of Paris. Cloth, 734 pages. One Dollar.

FROM CLOUDS TO SUNSHINE; OR, THE EVOLUTION OF A SOUL. By E. Thomas Kaven. Cloth, 12mo, 182 pages. One Dollar.

FROM THE FOUR WINDS. By Warren B. Hutchinson. Cloth, small 12mo. Fifty Cents.

GLEANINGS FROM NATURE. By Eva M. Carter. Cloth, 12mo. Illustrated. One Dollar.

GLOBE MUTINY, THE. By William Lay, of Saybrook, Conn., and Cyrus M. Hussey, of Nantucket. Cloth, 12mo, 163 pages. Seventy-five Cents.

"GOD AND THE CITY." By the Right Reverend Henry C. Potter, Bishop of New York. Paper, Ten Cents. A daintily printed, cloth bound edition, Twenty-five Cents.

GREAT BREAD TRUST, THE. By W. H. Wright. Cloth, Miniature Series, 54 pages. Fifty Cents.

GREATEST THING IN THE WORLD, THE. By Henry Drummond. Cloth, with photograph and biographical sketch of the author. Fifty Cents.

GREEN VALLEY. By T. P. Buffington. Cloth, 12mo, 151 pages. One Dollar.

GUMBO LILY, A. By Stella Gilman. Handsome Cloth, 12mo. Fifty Cents.

HALF HOUR STORIES. By Dora Harvey Munyon, A.M. Cloth, 12mo, 148 pages. One Dollar.

HALLIE MARSHALL. A True Daughter of the South. By F. P. Williams. Cloth, 12mo. One Dollar.

HANDFUL OF RHYMES, A. By Lischen M. Miller. Cloth, 12mo. $1.50.

HEALTH AND HYGIENE FOR THE HOUSEHOLD. By John Joseph Nutt. Cloth, Fifty Cents; paper, Twenty-five Cents.

ABBEY PRESS, 114 Fifth Ave., New York.

SOME PUBLICATIONS OF THE

HEART'S DESIRE, THE. "The Moth for the Star; The Night for the Morrow." By Barnetta Brown. Cloth (Miniature), daintily produced. Twenty-five Cents.

HEROINE OF SANTIAGO, THE; OR, WHAT FOLLOWED THE SINKING OF THE MERRIMAC. (A sequel.) By Antoinette Sheppard. Cloth, 12mo. One Dollar.

HER ROYAL HIGHNESS, WOMAN. By Max O'Rell. Cloth, 12mo. One Dollar.

HOCH DER KAISER. Myself und Gott. By A. McGregor Rose (A. M. R. Gordon). Fully illustrated by Jessie A. Walker. Second Edition. Cloth, 12mo. Fifty Cents.

HOUSE OF A TRAITOR, THE. By Prosper Merrimée. With photograph and biographical sketch of the author. Cloth. Fifty Cents.

HOW TO ENJOY MATRIMONY; OR, THE MONOGAMIC MARRIAGE LAW AMENDED BY TRIAL-EXPIRATION CLAUSE. By Rose Marie. Cloth. Twenty-five Cents.

HOW TOMMY WAS CURED OF CRYING. By Gertrude Mitchell Waite. Cloth, fully illustrated and daintily produced. Fifty Cents.

IN LOVE AND TRUTH. The Downfall of Samuel Seele, Healer. By Anita M. Muñoz. Cloth, 12mo. One Dollar.

INTELLECTUAL PEOPLE. By William Adolphus Clark. Fourth Edition. Cloth, small 12mo, 97 pages. Fifty Cents.

INTERNATIONAL DIRECTORY OF AUTHORS, THE. With a full list of their works, dates of publication, etc. Compiled and edited by Charles F. Rideal and Carlos Martyn. Cloth. $7.50. (In preparation.)

IRON HAND, THE. By Howard Dean. Cloth, 12mo. Illustrated. One Dollar.

ITURBIDE, A SOLDIER OF MEXICO. By John Lewin McLeish. Cloth, 12mo. Illustrated. One Dollar.

JEWELS OF PASTE. By Sue Edwards. Cloth, small 12mo. Fifty Cents.

JONAS BRAND; OR, LIVING WITHIN THE LAW. By Jane Valentine. Cloth, 12mo, 263 pages. One Dollar.

KEY-WORDS AND PHRASES OF THE NEW TESTAMENT. By the Rev. South G. Preston. Cloth, 12mo. One Dollar.

LADY OF MARK, THE. A Story of Frontier Experiences. By Sidney C. Kendall. Cloth, Fifty Cents.

LADY VERE. By L. M. Elshemus. Cloth, small 12mo, 126 pages. One Dollar.

LIFE'S SPRINGTIME. By J. N. Fradenburgh. Cloth, 12mo. One Dollar.

LIKE THE LILIES. By Lucy Tracy. Daintily Produced. Twenty-five Cents.

LIQUID FROM THE SUN'S RAYS. By Sue Greenleaf. Cloth, 12mo. $1.50.

LITERARY LIFE. (A monthly Illustrated Magazine.) Five Cents per copy or Fifty Cents per annum, mailed free.

LITTLE COURT OF YESTERDAY, A. By Minnie Reid French. Cloth, 12mo, 232 pages. One Dollar.

LITTLE CRUSADERS, THE. By Isabel Scott Stone. Cloth, 12mo. One Dollar.

LITTLE SCARECROW, THE. By Maurus Jokai. Cloth. Fifty Cents.

ABBEY PRESS, 114 Fifth Ave., New York.

SOME PUBLICATIONS OF THE

LODGING IN THE NIGHT, A. By Robert Louis Stevenson. Cloth. Fifty Cents.

LOST LOUISIANA, THE. By J. Kellogg. Cloth, 12mo. One Dollar.

LOVE AND PRIDE. By R. Rosino Napoliello. Cloth, 12mo. Fifty Cents.

LOVE'S RANDOM SHOT. By Wilkie Collins. Cloth. Fifty Cents.

MAGISTRACY, THE. Being a Directory and Biographical Dictionary of the Justices of the Peace of the United States. Compiled and edited by Charles F. Rideal and Carlos Martyn. (In preparation.)

MAN WITHOUT THE OATH, THE. By Olive C. Tobey. Cloth, 12mo, fully illustrated. One Dollar.

MASTER AND MAN. By Count Tolstoy. With photograph and biographical sketch of the author. Cloth. Fifty Cents.

MEN, WOMEN, AND LOVING. By Barnetta Brown. Cloth (Miniature), daintily produced. Twenty-five Cents.

MISS PENELOPE'S ELOPEMENT, AND OTHER STORIES. By Katherine Miles Cary. Cloth, small 12mo. Fifty Cents.

MISTAKES OF AUTHORS, THE. By Will M. Clemens. Cloth, 12mo. One Dollar.

MISTRESS OF MANY MOODS, A. Translated by Charlotte Boardman Rogers. Cloth, 12mo. Fifty Cents.

MUSICAL REFORMATION, A. By John A. Cone. Twenty-five Cents.

MYSTERY OF THE MARBLETONS, THE: A Romance of Reality. By M. Mackin. Cloth, 12mo. Fifty Cents. Small 12mo. Twenty-five Cents.

NARRAGANSETT PEER, THE. By George Appleton. Cloth, 12mo. One Dollar.

NEW DON QUIXOTE, THE. By Mary Pacheco. Cover design by C. H. Rowe. Cloth, 12mo. One Dollar.

NEW ENGLAND FOLK. By Mrs. C. Richmond Duxbury. Cloth, 12mo, 295 pages. One Dollar.

NEW SWISS FAMILY ROBINSON, THE. By Helen Pomeroy. Cloth, 12mo. One Dollar.

NEW THEORY OF EVOLUTION, A. By Alfred Ward Smith. Cloth, 12mo. $1.25.

NEW VERSION OF AN OLD STORY, A. By Elizabeth Milroy. One Dollar.

N'TH FOOT IN WAR, THE. By Lieut. M. B. Stewart, U. S. Army. Cloth, 12mo. Attractively designed cover. One Dollar.

OCTAVIA, THE OCTOROON A Southern Story. By J. F. Lee, M.D. Cloth, Fifty Cents.

OLD GLORY. By Lulu K. Eubank. Cloth, 12mo. Very fine. One Dollar.

ODD JEWEL, AN. A Postnuptial Tale of a World-wide Passion. By Warren M. Macleod. Cloth, small 12mo, 159 pages. Fifty Cents.

OLD GRAHAM PLACE, THE. By Etta M. Gardner. Cloth. Fifty Cents.

OLD SCHOOL DAYS. By Andrew J. Miller. Cloth, 12mo, 248 pages. One Dollar.

ONE THOUSAND WAYS TO MAKE MONEY. By Page Fox. Cloth, 12mo, 331 pages. One Dollar.

ON THE CHARLESTON. A Tale of the Taking of Guam. By Irene Widdemer Hartt. Cloth, 12mo, 289 pages. One Dollar.

ABBEY PRESS, 114 Fifth Ave., New York.

ND - #0139 - 060525 - C0 - 229/152/10 - PB - 9781333517366 - Gloss Lamination